On Their Way To

Donald Montgomery

Seanachaidh Publishing

SEANACHAIDH PUBLISHING LTD
Greenock, Scotland PA15 1BT
1989

Graphic Design by: William Stewart D.A.

ISBN 0-948963-55-7

Typeset by On-Line Text Ltd, Glasgow and
printed by Holmes MacDougall, Glasgow.

On Their Way To

LISBON

CONTENTS

Page

FOR BRENDA

Other works by the author:
(Plays)
Orlav's Helmet
This Desirable Residence

CHAPTER ONE

Paul Haddow would never forget the day his first child was born. It was the same day that Celtic drew Nil — Nil with Dulka Prague, the twenty fifth of April 1967.

Normally at seven o'clock in the evening Paul would have been taking his ease in the small flat he shared with his wife Anne Marie in Rutherglen, relaxing after the ardours of a hard day working in the sawmill at Polmadie.

Small and sturdy, Paul wore the well cut suit bought for his wedding six months previously. His youthful features were partially obscured by his longish, fashionably shaggy hair and a pair of heavy horn rimmed glasses. Paul had just turned twenty one but young and fit as he was, he puffed with the exertion of climbing the almost perpendicular slope of John Street, leading to the Royal Maternity Hospital in Rottenrow.

Paul was still simmering with excitement, barely able to believe the glad tidings, having only heard the good news less than an hour before. After all the waiting, the anxious sleepless nights and the torment of the endless afternoon, gradually in dazed delight, he realised the waiting was over, In Prague that afternoon Celtic had held the local side to a goalless draw to become the first British Club to reach the final of the European Cup.

He was also the father of a baby boy.

Two hours before this, three of Paul's friends had gathered in their usual corner of the Springfield Bar. The Springfield Bar was situated just off the Main Street in Rutherglen. The Spring, as it was known to its regulars, was a spartan, utilitarian hostelry. Its purpose, proclaimed over the door, was to dispense wines, beers and spirits. This it did to the entire satisfaction of its clientele. The dominating feature of The Spring was the traditional horseshoe bar, with a tempting variety of draught beers. Behind the bar stood an array of sparkling bottles on the well stocked gantry. For the greater comfort of its patrons, leather covered benches, upholstered with unyielding horsehair, ran along two of the perimeter walls. Several heavy trestle tables, partitioned one from the other by ornate oak panels, formed a series of open ended booths. Little daylight penetrated the dingy design on the high set tinted windows and the floor was stone, unadorned by any covering

5

save, when occasion demanded it, a sprinkling of sawdust. The Spring, as its habituees would smugly concede, was a man's pub.

In the corner booth, tacitly regarded as their own, sat Paul's friends, Desmond McNair and the O'Brien twins.

You would never have guessed that Desmond was a couple of years older than the twenty five year old twins. His fragile frame, haunched and pigeon chested, was a result of generations of deprivation. Buck teeth and close set eyes accentuated the customary melancholy of his expression. Serious by nature and, it has to be said, none too bright, Desmond looked at least ten years older than the O'Briens.

Perhaps the fact that Barney and Bill were still single had something to do with that. Desmond had married ten years earlier and laboured now under the yoke of his responsibilities. Desmond's family consisted of, two sons, two daughters and one wife. A postman by profession, his relaxation came from his nights out with the other Springfield regulars and an abiding lifelong passion for Glasgow Celtic.

The twins by comparison glowed with ruddy good health. Almost indistinguishable apart, each with the same carrot coloured crew cut, freckled face and button nose. Indulged to the point of killer kindness by their widowed mother, there were signs of their firmness turning to flab. Free from financial cares by virtue of well paid jobs as carpenters, Barney and Bill were among the more regular of the Springfield regulars.

The twins, who were currently involved in the construction of the new town of Cumbernauld, had forsaken their usual Tuesday night overtime and Desmond, who had just risen from his customary afternoon nap, strained to hear the commentary on the Celtic match.

From the battered radio on the bar came the genteel tones of BBC Scotland's top football commentator, George Davidson, in marked contrast to the raucous guttural ribaldry of the locals. It was obvious from the transmission, hollow and lacking in atmosphere, that his voice was coming to them, not from Czechoslovakia, but from in front of a television screen in Queen Margaret Drive, the BBC's Headquarters in Glasgow. Nevertheless, his description of the play held his audience spellbound until the final whistle.

The result was greeted uproariously by the bar's occupants and with as much abandon as they might have displayed at Parkhead, Celtic's stadium, situated about a mile or so down the road, or even at Hampden Park, the same distance away in the other direction.

In his customary place at the majestic gilt till, positioned at the end

6

of the gantry with a commanding view of the premises, stood Auld Tam, the manager of the Spring. In his early fifties and balding, Auld Tam regarded the jubilant customers and shrewdly computed his potential extra profit, his keg gnarled hands subconsciously caressing the great cash register as a musician might lovingly handle his instrument. Unlike most of the rejoicing Celtic fans who were Roman Catholics, Auld Tam was a Protestant, as a consequence of which he was, quite naturally, a supporter of Glasgow Rangers, Celtic's great rivals in the city. Not that Auld Tam would let a small matter like sectarian differences come between himself and an increased bonus — as far as he was concerned his till was interdenominational.

The Spring, unusually for that time on a Tuesday night, was alive with noise and excitement, the barmen hard pressed and Auld Tam's till tinkled through the clamour.

In the corner booth Desmond, who through lack of funds had been carefully nursing the pint he had bought at opening time, was generously treated by the elated twins.

"Ah canny get over it," wheezed Desmond, "Imagine Celtic in the European Cup Final." "Aye, who would have thought it?" said Barney. "There's no doubt about it," chipped in Bill, "Jock Stein's a genius."

Genius or not there was no doubting the effect the charismatic Mr Stein had had on Celtic. For years before his arrival they had floundered amongst the also-rans, but now under his astute guidance Celtic's star was high and rising, Solemnly the trio toasted Jock Stein. "It's fantastic when you think about it," said Desmond, "Ah mean we've got to the final at the first go. Look at Rangers, they've been in the European Cup three or four times." "Four" said Bill, setting the record straight. "Four times then," continued Desmond, "But the best they ever did wis to get to the semi-finals." "Aye, an' just the once at that," said Barney, eager to belittle the achievements of the Rangers.

"D'ye think we can win it?" asked Desmond, hardly daring to believe that such a miracle was imminently possible. "Accordin' to the papers we'll huv to go some," said Bill, "They're aye goin' on aboot thae big continental clubs like Real Madrid, Inter Milan an' that." "They've got a point there a' the same," said Desmond, "The Cup's been on the go now fur aboot eleven or twelve years." "Thirteen" Bill interrupted. "Well whitever it is," Desmond went on. "Ye canny argue wi' the fact that it's aye one o' thae furrin teams that wins it,"

This was no more than the truth, besides Rangers, Dundee, Hibs

7

and several star studded English sides had been thwarted in their attempts to capture the ultimate prize in inter club competition.

For a moment or two the trio considered this depressing fact, then Bill, with determined optimism, assessed the situation. "Look at it this way," he said, "It's no' only Celtic that's doin' well this season, it looks as though Rangers'll get to the final o' the Cup Winners Cup, — an' fur a' that we've got wur differences, Ah hope they do." The others nodded magnanimously. "An' whit aboot Kilmarnock?" Bill continued, "Ye would'nae huv given tuppence fur their chances o' reachin' the semi-finals o' the Fairs Cup. Ah mean to say, when ye think aboot it, three Scottish teams doin' well in the three top European competitions, it's good goin', is it no?"

Cheered by Bill's positive approach, not to mention the uplifting effects of another round of drinks, they eagerly cited other instances of Scotland's successes.

"An' jist to think," said Desmond, "That less than a year ago a' we got wis 'England this an' England that'. Ah wonder if they'll huv as much to say aboot us?" This was a reference to the saturation media coverage given to England's World Cup triumph the previous year. "Thon wis never a goal," growled Barney voicing the unanimous verdict of his fellow countrymen on the controversial and crucial third English goal in the final. This was the inevitable Scottish riposte to any mention of the Auld Enemy's success.

"Aye, but we showed them at Wembley this year," said Desmond. "Did we no' just?" said Bill gleefully, "Ye've seen nothing like Baxter an' Law that day, they crucified England."

The recent Scottish victory had been England's first defeat since winning the World Cup. The twins, who had been at Wembley, enthused at length on the Scots' display while all around them the football talk continued, excited groups speculated or reminisced, one story instantly capped by another, the heady combination of patriotism and alcohol charging their imaginations.

Amid the babble of conversation one word was heard with increasing frequency. That word was Lisbon.

It was going on for seven o'clock when the twins' mother, Mrs O'Brien, standing at the window of her terraced council house in Cambuslang Road, saw Joe Dolan come out of his mother's house which was next door.

Mrs O'Brien was of an older generation of unmistakeable Irish descent, old before their time, sober in apparel, their tired lined faces uncontaminated by cosmetics, their grey hair untainted by artificial colouring, regarding such frivolity as reprehensible if not downright sinful. A war widow, she had had a hard time bringing up her boys, and it showed.

Her head gently nodded in approval as she watched Joe skip down the path to the iron gate, set beside her own in the unruly hedge which separated the houses from the rush of traffic on the busy road.

Were it not terminologically impossible, Joe Dolan might well have been classed as the third O'Brien twin. Only a matter of weeks older than Barney and Bill, the three of them had started school together, been confirmed at the same service, celebrated their twenty-first birthdays with a joint party in the Co-operative Hall and at Joe's wedding Barney and Bill had shared the duties of Best Man. Mrs O'Brien had always been thankful for Joe's steadying influence on her wilder boys. She would endlessly cite Joe's example as a model for their aspirations, regardless of the fact that the twins made twice as much at their trade as Joe earned as a furnishing salesman in an Argyle Street store. Nevertheless, the fact that Joe went to work in a collar and tie commanded her utmost respect. Joe, furthermore, had in the eyes of Mrs O'Brien, elevated himself to the fringes of the aristocracy when he and his pretty wife, Betty, had bought their "ain hoose" up in Croftfoot. There was no doubt Joe Dolan was "gettin oan".

Joe was a fresh faced good looking lad with clear blue eyes and thick dark curly hair worn like a guardsman's busby. His youthful optimism was tempered with a mature gravity which, attractive in itself, gave greater credence to his sales spiels. It was by virtue of this serious vein and as as extension of his status as the twins' mentor, that Joe was tacitly held to be the leader of the Springfield regulars.

Mrs O'Brien watched in surprise as Joe, reverting to the habit of his less inhibited boyhood, vaulted the garden gate and danced off in the direction of Main Street. She was shocked by his uncharacteristic antics, but then Mrs O'Brien had not yet heard the result from Prague.

CHAPTER TWO

The Royal Burgh of Rutherglen is situated south of the River Clyde and, in common with other once self-contained communities within the Greater Glasgow boundary, is a much changed place since the mid-sixties.

The town nestles around the historic Main street, overlooked by the rolling tree crowned heights of the Cathkin Braes. At that time before the Civic Authorities re-developed the area, the old industrial sites and the tenement dwellings of the workers straggled towards the city on the west side, with the more affluent terraces and villas on the rising ground to the east.

When Desmond McNair emerged from the sorting room of the Post Office that fresh April morning following the birth of Paul's son, the tree lined Main Street still ran from the warren of tumbledown tenements situated at the Mill Street end, their grimy grey granite garishly brightened by the random collection of shops used by Livingston's Furnishings. Past this, going towards the Town Hall, the Main Street opened out like the estuary of a great river, the pavements broad, the road wide, and flanked by a satisfying variety of shops and stores from humble home bakers to the ubiquitous Woolworths. The Town Hall itself was, and still is, a wonderous pile. A granite eminence towering above the town, fairytale Gothic, surely more by accident than design, the peak of its tottering tower visible for miles around.

On leaving the Post Office, which was just past the Town Hall, Desmond crossed the road at the ancient Mercat Cross, a series of circular steps from which rises a slim pillar topped by a crouching lion. Desmond's back was bent with the weight of his morning deliveries. This was in addition to his usual burden, the cares of the world. He was, nevertheless thankful for the early morning sunlight after the dank dark winter months. It was not yet six o'clock, the few folks about silent and sleepy still. Only the sparrows, twittering deafeningly in the budding hawthorn and lime trees, disturbed the peace until, treating the otherwise deserted thoroughfare like the home straight at Le Mans, a red van from McGhee's Bakery thundered past, screeched suicidally into Farmloan Road and roared off towards Bridgeton.

Desmond, wisely perhaps, turned in the other direction up Stonelaw

10

Road and, as was his invariable habit, called in at Ali's General Store for his morning paper.

Ali's store was a claustrophobic emporium stocked from floor to ceiling with an unlikely range of merchandise. There was a pungent smell about the place, a mixture of camphor, dampness and oriental musk, distinctive certainly but not altogether unpleasant. On the counter to the right as you entered, squeezed between untidy heaps of household utensils, toys and dusty redundant periodicals, were piled the morning papers. Three bundles there were; the tabloid tower of "Daily Records" topping by a couple of inches the broadsheet edition of the "Daily Express" and for those with their minds on higher things, there was the sedate "Glasgow Herald".

At the back of the store, in a dim recess, the proprietor's fourteen year old daughter was preparing filled rolls, in conditions somewhat less than hygienic, for an impatient gaggle of girls bound for the early shift at Wills cigarette factory in Alexander Parade. Torn between two cultures, the Asian girl dispensed her duties huffily, treating the factory girls with a contempt tinged with envy.

Hidden from Desmond's view by a revolving display of pots and pans, Dunky McLinder searched among the stacked crates of lemonade for a bottle of Irn-Bru. The diminutive Dunky, five foot three in his crepe soled shoes, still favoured the fashions of the mid-fifties when he had had his adolescence. He was dressed now in drainpipe jeans with wide turn-ups, a full backed fingertip length jacket and a roary checked shirt worn loose at the neck. His hair protruded pompadour fashion over his brow and was slicked into a DA formation at the back, with the sideburns long and thick in the manner of a teddy-boy. Dunky was a popular figure in the community, renowned for his impudence and his quick Glasgow wit.

Ali, whose store it was, a dark eyed industrious immigrant from the sub continent, had been in the process of adding to the clutter in the shop by hanging up a net containing a number of footballs in the colours of the main Glasgow teams. As Desmond fumbled in his pockets for a ten shilling note, Ali continued with the task.

Dunky came to the counter at this point. "Ah see ye've got coloured balls Ali" he said straight faced. The cigarette girls giggled. Ali grinned, pleased his display had made an instant impression. "I am letting them hang out to be seen" he said, sending the girls into fits of raucous laughter. "Ye'd better watch yer heid, they near hit me" said an aggrieved Desmond looking round in bewilderment to see what might be amusing the Wills workers. He was still none the wiser when the girls, cackling and clutching rolls on spam or cheese rushed out to catch their bus.

Having finally located the errant note, Desmond collected a copy of the "Record", ten Number Six tipped and his change, then left the shop in the company of Dunky. Dunky scanned the back page of his "Express" which was dominated by news of Celtic's success. "Yer team's goin' great guns these days" he said to Desmond. "Aye they'll take some stoppin' now" Desmond replied, glowing with pride. "Ah dare say ye'll be goin' tae Lisbon for the final" said Dunky. The remark was made casually, a mere conversational gambit, but its effect on Desmond was electric. In the process of lighting a cigarette at the time Desmond froze. He stood transfixed until the burning match singed his fingers. "Ah hudnae thought aboot that" he said at length, then, still in a daze, he set off towards the large houses round Overtown Park.

Although he had missed few Celtic matches in the last twenty years and was now quite accustomed to visiting such remote footballing outposts as Aberdeen or Dumfries, or even on one memorable occasion, Liverpool, that was one thing, but Lisbon! Lisbon was different. Lisbon was abroad!

To Desmond "abroad" was a dimly perceived amalgam of conflicting images where half naked savages battled daily with fierce animals under a burning sun and returned at night to their wattle huts in the shadow of a great ivy covered castle, there to dine, squatting on the rush covered floor, on snakes, snails and frogs. "Abroad" was distant and exotic. "Abroad" was no place for the likes of Desmond McNair. And yet . . .

Desmond trudged up the road deep in thought, his brow furrowed by the unaccustomed effort, his cigarette still dangling from his lips, as yet unlit.

Amused by the effect his chance remark had had on Desmond, Dunky McLinder smiled as the postman departed, then turned his attention to the bottle of Irn Bru, the amber effervescent mineral water, justifiably claimed by its manufacturers to be Scotland's other national drink. Unceremoniously, Dunky tipped half the contents down his throat, waited for the belch which didn't come, then set off home, turning into Main Street at Boots the Chemist.

It was evident from the stubble on his chin which in these days was

12

called a five o'clock shadow, that, unlike most of the others out and about at that early hour, Dunky ws unemcumbered by the strictures of conventional employment. A free wheeling spirit, officially unemployed, Dunky supplemented his "buroo money" with a variety of odd jobs, and in his opinion, shrewd investments at William Hills. It had been more than eight years since his last official job, as a delivery driver for a local firm, which had been terminated when he had advised an important client to, (in effect) fornicate elsewhere.

Thus, free from inhibiting routine, Dunky was able to follow the impulse of the moment, to go where chance might take him. He had left home the previous evening with no clear intentions and had become involved in a protracted card school. This was not unusual for Dunky who had been known to be absent from home for days at a time in similar circumstances. His night's work to judge from his jaunty step, had been more rewarding than most.

Dunky smirked impishly up at the row of censorious concrete saints eternally scrutinising the passing populace from the sooty red brick facade of St Columbkill's Chapel. Continuing past the Odeon cinema he turned into Mill Street where his pace slackened perceptively.

Carefree and careless as he was, Dunky McLinder, like all male mortals had eventually to answer to a greater authority. In a third floor flat in one of the crumbling tenements, which at that time stood in Mill Street, resided Dunky's ultimate sanction, Big Bella.

Logic would suggest that at some time Big Bella had been Wee Bella, but logic in this case had to be augmented by a lively imagination. Big Bella appeared to have been hewn from a solid chunk of granite by an enthusiastic but inept sculptor. Broad in the beam, full breasted, arms and fists like hams, Big Bella was a fearsome sight when raised to wrath, which was more often than not.

For a fleeting moment in the metamorphosis from Wee Bella to Big Bella, her fiery spirit and a pretty snub nose had given her sufficient allure to attract and snare the unwary Dunky, who had never heard the advice of Dr Johnson, and made the mistake of marrying the whole woman. Her dark hair drawn severely back into a french roll, the pretty nose now a bulbous blob above her cavernous mouth, Big Bella was awesome to behold.

"An jist whit sort o' time d'ye ca' this tae come home?" bellowed the lady of the house. "Gie's a break Bella, Ah'm tired" Dunky pleaded to no avail. "Tired" Bella exploded, "Your're tired? You're no' the only one that's tired in this house. Ah'm sick an' tired waitin'

13

here like a dooly till it suits you tae come home. Let me tell you . . ." Big Bella went on, and on, and on.

Since there was little else he could do in the face of this onslaught, Dunky took it bravely, looking suitably contrite.

Undeterred by the entrance of their two children, Bella ranted, raved and roared for half an hour or more. The children were well used to their parents' ways. Nine year old Ronnie stoically prepared his breakfast cereal and, immune to the raging storm, perused the strip cartoon stories in the "Broons Book".

Senga, a twelve year old clone of her mother, regarded the proceedings through narrowed eyes, arms akimbo, listening and learning. Somewhere at that moment an embrionic Dunky was innocently enjoying his breakfast unaware of what fate held in store.

At some point during Bella's outburst, Dunky slipped a couple of five pound notes into a jug, inscribed as "a present from Portobello" which stood on the mantelpiece. Bella deigned not to notice but shortly after her rage subsided to anger, her turn of phrase, which until then had been vitriolic, was now merely caustic. The storm had passed.

Senga, keen to demonstrate her womanly ways, then berated her brother for reading at the table, cuffed him about the ears and snatched away the offending annual. Ronnie with an optimism unjustified by his record in such encounters, noisily contested her possession. The household was thus restored to a state of normality.

Although, in her own words, Bella might "go on till she was blue in the face", there was little likelihood of her changing Dunky's ways, but she at least derived a degree of satisfaction from these outbursts. Dunky for his part enjoyed indulging his wanderlust no matter the consequences.

Some marriages are made in heaven.

At about the same time as the McLinders were settling their differences, a haunched hollow eyed Paul Haddow waited ouside the Odeon Cinema for his customary lift to work in a workmate's car. His brown boiler suit, work soiled jacket and ungainly but practical industrial boots were in marked contrast to the dapper figure of the previous evening. Paul was recognisable only by his distinctive horn rimmed glasses.

Slouched disconsolately against the tile entrance to the picture house the beauty of the spring morning was wasted on Paul. This was the morning after the day he would never forget.

The night before Paul had visited the Maternity Hospital, been reunited with his wife and had held his son for the first time. Paul had then, as is the custom on these occasions, called in at the Spring. His arrival as it turned out was timely, the celebration of Celtic's victory was running out of steam. Desmond had already left and Joe Dolan and the twins were on the point of departure. Paul was greeted enthusiastically, a fresh round of drinks were ordered, then another. The lads were normally beer drinkers, McEwans Heavy by preference but, as befitted the occasion and to the benefit of Auld Tam's bonus, one whisky followed another. In traditional fashion the baby's head was well and truly wetted.

When chucking out time came at ten past ten, Paul had risen in a dwam there were now four red headed O'Briens and the door had somehow been transferred from one side of the pub to the other.

Paul, it is certain, would never have got home that night without the help of Joe Dolan. Joe, a canny creature, had long since learned that it was possible to have an enjoyable evening without drinking to the point of stupification.

Unfortunately, the same could not be said of the twins who had been drinking since opening time. Amazingly they nevertheless demonstrated an innate ability to defy the law of gravity. This was achieved by one clinging to the other as he was about to subside. This method was successful as long as the twins shared at least one steady leg between them. Miraculously in this manner they made the half mile journey home.

Joe, not without difficulty, had taken Paul home, put him to bed and, being an organised person himself, had set Paul's alarm for the morning.

Through hungover eyes, Paul saw the Morris Minor Estate coming towards him. Moving to the kerb, his head throbbed. His workmate grinned knowingly but unsympathetically as they set off past the War Memorial. Slumped in the passenger seat, Paul reflected philosophically that things could be worse. Mother and child were both doing well and Celtic had won. Apart from the hammer blows to his brain occasioned by the least movement, there was only one cloud on his horizon. He and his wife, Anne Marie, had been unable to come to an agreement on a name for the new born child.

15

CHAPTER THREE

The following Saturday was Cup Final Day in Scotland and inevitably Celtic were involved.

After the excesses of the Tuesday evening it was Saturday night before any of the lads had the stomach or the money to visit the Spring. Many of the Spring's other regulars were in the same boat, consequently Auld Tam's bonus was looking prospectively less healthy.

It had long been the custom that the lads met in the Spring on Saturdays between six and seven thirty. The twins, Desmond and Paul would normally have been at the Celtic match in the afternoon and Joe would call in on his way home from a busy day at the store. Although Joe now had every third Saturday off, it still meant he missed more games than any loyal fan should.

Desmond was the first to arrive. Desmond looked troubled. Ever since Wednesday morning when Dunky's chance remark had set into cumbersome motion his rusty thought processes, Desmond had been alternately thrilled and horrified at the thought of travelling to Lisbon to see Celtic in the final. "Ur ye goin'?" had been the inevitable opening gambit at Hampden that afternoon and all over Scotland the supporters' clubs had started to make their arrangements.

The Celtic team, as it had all season, responded to the mood of the moment, the men in the famous green and white jerseys had once again turned in a superlative performance. Aberdeen had been beaten two — nil, both goals being scored by the patriotically named Willie Wallace, taking the Scottish Cup to Parkhead to stand beside the League Cup captured earlier in the season.

The twins arrived sharply dressed in well cut suits, as sturdy and good looking lads as any mother would want for their daughter. Though neither of them had been caught in this trap so far, if they had thought about it both would have accepted it as inevitable. Even now Bill was due to meet Sheena a girl he had gone out with off and on since their schooldays, and Barney had a date "wi' a lassie fae Castlemilk, a right wee doll". Barney and his wee doll were going to the jazz club at Shawfield Stadium that night.

"Whit aboot you lot? Ur youse goin'?" Auld Tam shouted the question amid the boozy fug and bustle of the Saturday night throng, but was then immediately distracted by a rush from the other side of the bar. "Ah'd love tae" Desmond mournfully informed the twins. "Well whit's stoppin' ye?" asked Barney. "It's no' that easy," sighed Desmond, "It's a' right for the likes o' youse, but ah've got ma wife an' weans to think about." "Ah'm sure Jean'll no' mind," said Bill, "She's never stopped ye goin' tae see Celtic afore." "Aye but they've never played in Lisbon afore," said Desmond, "Ah don't even know where Lisbon is," "Lisbon is the capital city of Portugal," interjected Joe who had just arrived, "A busy seaport on the banks of the Tagus an' one o' the two main football teams, Sportin' Lisbon play in — wait fur it — green and white stripes." Barney was impressed, "How d'ye know a' that stuff" Bill too, "Ah wish Ah'd stuck in mair at the school" he said. Joe laughed and held up the pink Saturday night football special, "It's a' here in the "Times" the night" he said.

When Paul joined them in the corner booth soon after, the regular quintet was complete. "Ur ye goin'?" Desmond asked Paul. "No, there's no visitin' on a Saturday night," he replied mistaking the question, then added, scowling over his glasses, "The visitin' is in the efternoon on a Saturday. Is that no daft?" Paul was disappointed at having missed the Cup Final. "Ye missed a rare game," said Bill, rubbing it in.

"What Desmond meant," explained Joe, "Wis ur ye thinkin' aboot goin' tae the European Cup Final." Paul was taken aback. Since Tuesday his life had been a non-stop round of hospital visits and work. He had had other matters to think about, not least the vexing question of the baby's name.

"Ur youse?" Paul said eventually. "Ah'd love to," said Desmond. "Me too" from Bill, "An me," said his twin. "Then why don't we go?" said Joe, "We'd a' like tae be there, so whit's stoppin us?"

Another couple of rounds were bought in while the pros and cons were examined. Wives and weans would have to be considered, so too would be the time they would have to take off work and then there was the small matter of the cost. To Desmond in particular these obstacles had seemed insurmountable, but by the time the fifth round had arrived the mood of the party had changed. What indeed was there to stop them? Desmond's family could enjoy themselves just as much for a week at Blackpool as for two. Paul's wife, Anne Marie, would be fully occupied with the new baby and, they persuaded themselves, would be happier if Paul was out of the way for a while. Joe's main concern was the problem of getting time off work but the twins were determined to go come what may.

The mood had become euphoric until Bill, a tremor in his voice revealing a deep felt fear, asked: "Do we huv to go in an airyplane?" Joe smiled a surprised and superior smile. "Ye're no' worried aboot that ur ye?" he asked, then once again indicating the pink 'Times", "There's nothin' to it, we can get one o' they charter flights fur aboot twenty quid." Desmond gasped, not from fear of flying, twenty pounds was more than a week's wages. Barney shared his brother's concern about flying. "Ah've never been in a plane afore", he said.

"Ah've flew twicst," said Desmond surprising everyone and, to his great discomfort, suddenly becoming the centre of attention. "When was this?" asked Paul. "D'ye no' mind? When me an' Jean got married we flew tae the Isle of Man." "Whit wis it like?" asked Bill. "Ah quite enjoyed it" replied Desmond, "There wis a nice wee pub just alang fae the Villa Marina." Resisting the impulse to clout him, Joe simplified the question. "We're no' interested in the Isle O' Man, we want to know what it wis like flyin'." "Ach there's nothin' to it," said Desmond now enjoying the impression of sophistication he was creating, conveniently forgetting his own misgivings at the time.

"When wis the second time?" demanded Paul. "Whit d'ye mean?" asked Desmond dimly, tarnishing the image of the experienced aviator. "Ye said ye'd flew twice" said Paul. "Twicst", Joe corrected him. "That's right," agreed Bill, "Ye telt us ye flew tae the Isle O' Man on yer honeymoon, when wis the other time?" Desmond looked at the ring of inquisitive faces and wondered just how daft folks could get. "We flew back again" he said. Leaving the others speechless.

Soon after this, the twins left to meet their girlfriends, but not before it had been agreed that Joe would look into the travel arrangements and report back.

The topic of conversation then changed to belated enquiries after the health of mother and child. "Huv ye got a name for that wean yet?" asked Joe. Paul, who had been enjoying himself, now snorted with disgust. "Aye," he said "It's to be Kenneth." "Whit's wrong wi' that?" asked Joe. Paul sighed, "Ah'd wanted to ca' him efter one o' the Celtic players" he said. Joe looked to Desmond who, not normally noted for his erudition, had an encyclopaedic knowledge of matters pertaining to Celtic Football Club. Desmond thought for a moment before he responded. "We've got a boy on the books ca'ed Kenneth" he said "Kenny Dalglish, he's no' bad they tell me." Joe gave Paul a consoling pat on the shoulder, "There ye are," he said, "he's got a

18

Celtic player's name efter all." "Big deal," grunted Paul ungraciously, "Ah wanted to name him after Bertie Auld or Steve Chalmers, who's ever heard o' Kenny Dalglish?"

CHAPTER FOUR

The more the lads thought about going to Lisbon the more they realised it could be done. Hopes were high then and rising. But inevitably there were complications and opposition to the proposed trip came from an unexpected quarter.

Anne Marie and baby Kenneth had been discharged from the hospital on the Sunday. This involved a hectic few days for her mother, her sisters and, not least, for her husband.

Anne Marie was a pretty nineteen year old, her elfin face framed by long fair hair worn straight and simple. But it was Anne Marie's legs which were her most striking feature. It was her great fortune that the introduction of the mini-skirt had coincided with her flowering, and Anne Marie was seldom seen out of doors in anything other than the skinny figure hugging sweaters then in vogue and the skimpiest of skirts, revealing to the fullest extent her long and lovely legs. Desirable as she was however, it was generally agreed that Anne Marie had been given her beauty as compensation for her lack of grey matter. Vague and scatterbrained, Anne Marie sallied uncaring through life, improvident to the extreme and totally lacking in foresight. Consequently when she arrived home from hospital, it fell to the womenfolk of her family to rally round and provide the essential requisites for the baby. Simple things like clothing, nappies, bottles and even a cot. Anne Marie had of course meant to have all these things in, but had somehow just not got round to it.

It was Wednesday night before Anne Marie and Kenneth were suitably provided for. For the meantime at least. That night Celtic were due to play Dundee United at Parkhead. The game had a special significance since, if Celtic won, they would acquire the two points necessary for them to clinch the League Championship. Naturally the lads were at the game.

Realising that this was as good a time as any, Desmond's wife Jean called in to see Anne Marie with a "wee mindin' for the wean".

Jean was a small timid woman who, apart from promising to love,

19

honour and obey Desmond in her marriage vows, appeared also to have agreed to help him with the burden of the world's cares. At ease only in the comfort of her own home, Jean was fretful and unsure in company, her lined features perpetually perturbed and with a nervous habit of pushing imaginary wisps of her untidy greying hair off her broad forehead.

When Jean arrived she was shown into the small kitchen. Mrs O' Brien, the twins' mother and Betty Dolan, Joe's wife were already there.

Since their hastily arranged marriage, six months previously, Paul and Anne Marie had been living in a rented room and kitchen flat in Mitchell Street. Until the baby's arrival, this accommodation had been regarded by the young couple as a cosy love nest. Now, although in the past many a struggling mother had borne and reared large families in similar circumstances, Paul and Anne Marie were deemed officially to be overcrowded and were hoping to be rehoused in the newer Council housing scheme at Fernhill.

It was on this subject that Mrs O' Brien was holding forth when Jean came in. Notwithstanding the presence of her hostess and the other younger women, Mrs O' Brien was complaining about the mollycoddling of today's youth and comparing their lot with the rigours she had endured as a young widow and mother during the war. Betty Dolan, her expression smug and superior, nodded sagely, she was in complete agreement with the older woman.

Joe's wife was attractive in a prim sort of way, tastefully but not extravagantly dressed, her pretty face haloed by a boufant mass of auburn hair. A mere twenty two years old, Betty was thought of as conceited, self opinionated and snobbish, all of which was, unfortunately true. Sad to say, Betty Dolan was a pain in the neck.

The lack of enterprise and self control in some of her contemporaries was one of Betty's favourite themes. Rudely breaking into Mrs O' Brien's discourse, Betty expounded her own theories at length. The fact that young couples with no more foresight than had Paul and Anne Marie, could acquire a house and garden with little or no effort of their own, could only distort their sense of values. Betty was equally forthright on the question of children. Betty and Joe had both worked hard to "get where they were" as she put it. Only two rooms of the house at Croftfoot were furnished and until such times as Betty decided that they were "on their feet" there would be no thought of adding to the Dolan dynasty.

Mrs O'Brien, a Catholic mother of the old school, sat through the latter part tight lipped. On the other hand, Jean, however much she disliked Betty and was uncomfortably aware of Mrs O'Brien's disapproval, guiltily wished she had been more knowledgeable about these matters earlier in her own marriage. Although once started Betty needed little encouragement, Jean felt a nod or the occasional "Oh aye" were called for. Sadly her efforts went unnoticed by Betty and only fueled Mrs O'Brien's indignation, thereby adding to Jean's own discomfort.

Anne Marie had heard it all before and had had sufficient foresight to put on the kettle while Betty was talking. When she began serving the tea things the topic of conversation had turned to the proposed Lisbon trip. "Ah canny say ah'm keen on the idea," Mrs O'Brien said, "But if that's whit they want then ah'm sure ah'll no be able to stop them." Jean, feeling on safer ground on this subject, timidly put in her twopence worth; "Desmond's fair lookin' forward to it, so he is." Surprisingly, Betty was now the one with the tight lips. "Huv one o' thae Tunnock's carmel wavers" cajoled Anne Marie, holding the plate towards Betty. "Really, I don't think it's good enough!" Betty pronounced primly. "What d'ye want? Caviar?" exclaimed Anne Marie, outraged by the apparent criticism of her hospitality. Betty's lips relaxed sufficiently to allow a grim smile of condescension. "No, no Anne Marie" Betty excused himself, "That's not what I meant at all. But if you don't mind I'll just hiv one o' thae wee Abernethys." Betty took the shortcake. "Ur ye sure ye'll no' huv a carmel waver? They're Paul's favourite" said Anne Marie. Betty explained with a virtuous air "Really, thanks but no thanks. You see me an' Joe decided not to indulge in needless luxuries like chocky bickies until such times as we find wur feet." Betty favoured the company with a brave smile. "Please yersel'." shrugged her hostess and bit noisily into one of the carmel wafers.

Demurely nibbling her Abernethy, the frugal Betty expanded on her previous statement "I must say that I disapprove entirely of this Lisbon nonsense." Mrs O' Brien, who had been happy enough to let her boys go in the knowledge that Joe would be there too, was alarmed. "D'ye mean Joe's no' goin'? she asked. Jean was shocked into a further contribution to the conversation. 'Oh my!" she said genuinely concerned. Anne Marie had been rendered speechless because her mouth was full."Fur why's Joe no' goin'?" she demanded. Not having entirely digested her biscuit her question was accompanied by a fine spray of crumbs.

Betty listened to their comments with a stoic and superior calm, only a slight tightening of her mouth and an almost imperceptible twitch of her pert pointed nose indicated that she had noticed Anne Marie's visible contribution. Speaking with an irksome whine, Betty coolly defined her opposition. Having got where they were by dint of hard work and regular saving, she had no intention of letting her Hubbie — ("Hubbie!" Mrs O' Brien's tea went down the wrong way, Jean blinked, mouth agape and Anne Marie grimaced in disgust.) — of letting her Hubbie go charging about the continent like some latter day coeur de Lion, (Like a whit?" Anne Marie mouthed to the others) and besides there was his career to think of. (Other husbands had jobs, Joe had a career.) Not that she would ever deny Joe his pleasures up to a point, but a line had to be drawn somewhere. And had any of them thought about the cost of this junket?

Until now Betty had had it all her own way but now she had gone too far. Did she think she was the only one with financial commitments? Jean surprised them all including herself by voicing her opinions. Jean well knew the value of money and regularly worked wonders with Desmond's wage packet. Content as he was if he had enough to follow Celtic and pay for his round in the Springfield on a Saturday night, Desmond had never been a curse on her purse like other husbands she could name. Scrimping and saving there would be but, whatever the cost, as far as Jean was concerned, Desmond would go to the game.

Mrs O'Brien had had some misgivings about the amount involved. She had struggled to rear her boys and could well remember when even a day trip to Ayr or Largs had been a severe strain on the family's resources. Her innate monetary caution cavilled at the extravagance, nevertheless the boys worked hard for their money and deserved to reap the reward. Bill and Barney would be going.

Anne Marie needless to say hadn't thought about it at all. If Paul wanted to trail hundreds of miles to see Celtic that was his business and he was welcome to do so.

Betty was taken aback by this show of strength. With less conviction than before she continued to raise objections until, realising she was getting nowhere, she finished lamely with the remark that it was only a silly football match after all.

Her audience gasped, the ultimate blasphemy had been uttered, Only a football match!

The others had always known that Betty was different. After all

22

before her marriage she had come from Shawlands and she had always been a bit uppity, but for Joe's sake they put up with her. But to suggest that this match or any other game in which Celtic were involved was only a silly football match!

Generations of Glaswegian womenfolk on both sides of the sectarian divide had been raised to realise the wisdom of Bill Shankly's words: Football wasn't a matter of life or death, it was much more important than that.

Betty was on her own, any reservations Anne Marie, Jean or Mrs O' Brien had had were now dismissed.

With nothing further to discuss and baby Kenneth crying to be fed, the soiree broke up. Mrs O' Brien left to overfeed the twins and Jean scuttled off to the sanctuary of her own familiar fireside.

Betty, her composure bruised and battered, departed in ignominy. Only a football match indeed!

CHAPTER FIVE

The meeting of the womenfolk at Anne Marie's home took place on the Wednesday. On the Friday Dunky McLinder lost his shaving brush. A small matter you might say but as far as the longterm plans of the Springfield regulars were concerned, it was to have far reaching consequences.

Dunky was puzzled by the disappearance of the shaving brush. The McLinder home, while never a showpiece, was normally clean and tidy. Credit where it's due, Big Bella was conscientious in her housework and woe betide anyone who disrupted her orderly realm. As it turned out it was young Ronnie to blame. He had apparently been practising shaving as a distraction on a wet afternoon and had failed to restore the shaving brush to its customary postion. It had taken Dunky ten minutes to find it, ten fateful minutes as it transpired.

Ten minutes of course were nothing to Dunky whose life was free from the shackles of routine, but had it not been for that crucial delay Dunky would have been out and about before his wife had been bound for her normal round of the shops, clutching the stout leather shopping bag which was used daily to convey all the necessary provisions for the household. No weekly trip to the supermarket for Bella, no family car to transport her purchases. Big Bella, as

23

generations of wives and mothers before her had done, daily augmented her household stores, patiently queuing for each item in a succession of specialist shops.

Unusually therefore the McLinders were seen in tandem, sallying forth into Main Street, Dunky, mentally shrugging off the option of desertion, dug his hands deep into the pockets of his jeans, grinned cheekily up at his gargantuan spouse and philosophically accepted fate's eccentric decree.

Big Bella for her part felt irked and inhibited by the unaccustomed presence of her husband. Dunky's leisurely pace contrasted with her own determined gait, making it necessary for her to adjust, otherwise Dunky would have been left, as other mortals were, in the wake of her great bulk. Big Bella was disadvantaged, she was not accustomed to making concessions.

Dunky's progress along Main Street, as indeed was his progress anywhere, was punctuated by flippant and irreverent remarks, many of which Bella had heard often enough before. Nevertheless, his efforts were rewarded by amused smiles from his wife and even on one occasion, outright laughter.

When, for example they were passing a shop which was temporarily closed for alterations and there was stuck on the grimy window the usual dire warning to the effect that if advertising material was placed on the glass, legal proceedings would be taken, Dunky's inevitable comment was: "Ah would'nae like to be Bill Posters when they catch him." Bella remembered this one from her courting days. She smiled.

"Ah see they've got their knickers doon in the Co'." said Dunky, nodding towards an advertisement in the window of the Co-operative Department Store proclaiming reductions in the lingerie department.

In the queue at the City Bakeries a tall well dressed woman with an air of self-satisfied superiority was in front of the McLinders. "Wan o' thae would-be toffs frae Burnside," Bella confided to Dunky, attempting a whisper but failing by a score of decibels or more. The tall woman stiffened, then asked the assistant for a small brown loaf. "We've nane left at the moment," said the shop girl "But the driver's comin' back wi' some more." "How long will they be?" asked the tall woman. "Aboot ten inches, same as usual," chipped in Dunky, to the amusement of all except the tall woman, who stormed from the shop in disgust. Dunky and Bella were enjoying themselves.

Outside Woolworths the unusually happy couple met Annie Marie

24

pushing her pram. That Bella should have anything at all to do with Anne Marie was testament to a tolerant streak in Bella's nature.

Anne Marie, Paul and most of their friends were Roman Catholics. Big Bella on the other hand had been strictly reared in that peculiar tradition inherited from her immigrant Ulster ancestors, rabid Orange men and women who held that anything to do with Roman Catholicism or the Pope, their arch enemy, was the work of the devil. Big Bella was a fervent disciple of the movement and like others of her kind paraded regularly behind dowdy banners and clamorous accordians, flutes and drums. Swearing lifelong allegiance to the Queen, passionately supporting Glasgow Rangers and never eating fish on a Friday.

Self appointed defenders of the Protestant faith who, weddings and baptisms apart, were never seen inside a church. Anne Marie, however, had for many years before her marriage lived up the same close as the McLinders. Bella was fond of the girl and conceded "Ach, she's no' a bad lass, it's no' her fault she's a Catholic."

Inevitably, baby Kenneth was the centre of attraction, the women oohing and aahing over the mite. "Wid ye jist look at that!" Big Bella cooed, "Whit d'ye think Dunky, Is he no' the spit o' his father?" Dunky had cunningly contrived a position from which, reflected in Woolworth's darkened window, he could admire the rear view of Annie Marie bending over the pram. Reluctantly, he focused on Kenneth. "So he is an' a'," he agreed with his wife, "A' he needs noo is a pair o' Hank Marvin specs." Cheerfully Dunky slipped a half crown under the baby's pillow in the traditional manner.

In the course of the ensuing conversation, the McLinders learned of the proposed trip to Lisbon which was now threatened by a further setback. Such had been the demand that the airline companies had substantially increased the cost of the flight, putting the project back in the melting pot. Dunky observed that little more could be expected of the airlines since they were run by a bunch of fly men. Bella's scowl at this remark was hint enough to Dunky that their unaccustomed period of accord was drawing to a close, so when the women went into Boots the Chemist Dunky set off towards Farm Cross for no better reason than that this was the way he had been facing.

CHAPTER SIX

On Saturday 6 May Rangers played Celtic at Ibrox Park. This was an important match for several reasons. In the first instance, to their respective followers, all Old Firm games are important but in addition to this Rangers had emulated their rivals by reaching the final of the European Cup Winners Cup on the previous Wednesday. On that same evening, Celtic met Dundee United needing only one point to win the league Championship.

The Parkhead faithful had turned out in force for the last game of the season at Celtic Park. At the interval Celtic were leading by a goal to nil, the Scottish Cup was triumphantly paraded round the ground to rapturous acclaim. Forty five minutes later the super Celts left the field to muted applause. The match was won by Dundee United by three goals to two. In an otherwise all conquering season, Celtic had been beaten home and away by the Tayside team.

Two league matches remained to gather that one important point, only one side could pip Celtic to the post and that team inevitably was Rangers. But Rangers would have to win this game which was the traditional New Year's Day confrontation which had been postponed until now. No finer finale could have been planned.

The Old Firm match, Rangers versus Celtic is regarded in Scotland as the greatest club match in the world. They may think differently in Liverpool, Manchester or even Buenos Aires but there is no doubt that with its unique ingredient of belligerent religious bigotry, the Glasgow derby is an awesome occasion.

On that rain sodden May afternoon in 1967 a neutral observer who had never previously witnessed an Old Firm clash, and whose perspective was unsullied by any preconceived prejudices of his own, would have observed scenes of ritual tribal rivalry without parallel in the sporting world.

Ibrox Park has seen many changes since that day, only the main stand with its distinctive cross hatched ledge on the upper tier remains. Across from the stand was an antiquated but adequate covered enclosure and to the left, distanced from the playing field by the broad perimeter running track, rose a vast uncovered terrace, Behind the goal at the opposite end was a similar high terrace but with the added

26

refinement that it was protected from the elements for the most part by a new cantilever cover.

Since only in the main stand was there any seating accommodation, our neutral observer should have taken his seat there at least forty minutes before the kick off. By this time he would have been aware of the voluntary segregation of the fans. It would be evident to the most innocent of bystanders that the exposed terrce to his left was the Celtic end. Even at this early stage the green and white favoured fans would be making their presence felt regardless of the incessant rain. To his right the Rangers end would be filling rapidly with their fervent support, sporting their colours of red, white and blue. The diehard followers of both clubs gathered behind the goal areas, more rational but no less committed souls occupied the central covered enclosure.

Refreshed in the city's hostelries and made bold by the proximity of likeminded zealots and the comfortable distance which separated the rival fans, the crowd were soon ready to open the afternoon's proceedings. From the Rangers' end, orchestrated by an invisible choirmaster, several thousand voices simultaneously burst into song. "Hallo! Hallo! We are the Billy boys," a cordial salutation directed towards the fans at the Celtic end.

From the left the Celtic following responded with a lively chorus of "Hail! Hail! The Celts are here". Mutual introductions complete the Celtic choir modulated into a spirited rendition of "Soldiers are we". This was followed by a tuneful selection from the fans opposite; "Derry's Walls", "The Sash" and "There's Not a Team Like the Glasgow Rangers". The reply from the Parkhead faithful was loud, proud and clear. Theirs, they passionately averred, was "A Grand Old Team to Play For".

Our neutral observer unaware of the hate and malice engendered by and incorporated in these sectarian anthems, and marvelling at their apparent spontaneity, would no doubt have enjoyed this traditional exchange.

As the kick off time approached the singing increased in passion and in volume, interruped only by the crackling of the public address system. The rival chants were momentarily stilled for the announcer with the seemingly indispensable attribute for the job, common to his fellows the world over, nasal congestion. Despite this handicap he commanded the rapt attention of the multitude. "Hood afterdoon," he boomed, "Here are today's finhal team selectshuns."

27

At five to three, led out by their respective captains, the teams appeared. Rangers, resplendent in their V-necked royal blue jerseys, followed John Greig, stern and strong, the epitomy of indomitable courage and determination acknowledged by friend and foe alike, as one of the truly great Rangers. Equally valiant and steadfast, Billy McNeil, grim and unyielding, the personification of the Parkhead tradition, captained the Celts.

As three o'clock and the kick off approached, the cacophony of sound, the intensity of the hate and the passion increased. Blood boiled, adrenaline flowed, seventy eight thousand throats roared their undying allegiance according to religious persuasion or prejudice. The players, their senses battered by the unrelenting clamour, were spurred to even greater determination and who would have blamed the referee if he then wished he had been safely at home with his solitary parent.

There are some who hold that the football is only incidental on these occasions, it is the result, no matter the manner of its achievement, which is paramount. In the history of these clashes it is surprising how few actual games are remembered in themselves only match winning goals, individual performances and of course, villainous deeds are recalled in detail. But in that particular confrontation, with all to play for and European glory beckoning, both sides excelled. Despite the inclement weather and the unseasonable May mud, there was an abundance of exciting end to end play with no quarter asked or given and countless goalmouth incidents.

Spectacularly, with half time approaching, Rangers took the lead. From our neutral observer's vantage point the scene was incredible. One end of the stadium was as animated and exultant as the other was silent and stilled. To his right, the joyful host in red, white and blue roared their approval. The seething mass delirious with delight. Scarves were brandished, Union Jacks unfurled, grown men embraced and primitive gestures of supremacy were directed at the sullen sodden fans behind the opposite goal.

Sensationally, within a minute, the positions were reversed when Celtic scored to level the game. The elated hoards to the left of our neutral observer, celebrated in frenzied ecstasy. Pat hugged Mick and the gold, green and white republican tricolour was flaunted. Such instant retribution was doubly sweet, faith was restored.

Their jubilation cut off in its prime, the fans at the Rangers' end were momentarily stunned to silence but quickly rallied behind their favourites. "We'll support you evermore" they sang as the Parkhead contingent gleefully countered with "We'll walk a million miles for one of your goals" The din continued even when the players went in at half time.

In the second half the singing, the excitement and the downpour continued. Despite the atrocious conditions, and watched by representatives of their prospective opponents in the European competitions, the teams performed with grit, determination and no small measure of skill. It was an exhilerating exhibition of the kind of football we may never see again, relying on the traditional Scottish virtues of good wing play.

Four internationalist wingers were on show that day, masters of their craft and entertainers all. Wee Willie Henderson was supreme on the Rangers' right, small and skilful, but his wily runs and deft crosses were emulated by his opposite number in the Celtic side, the irreplaceable jinking Jimmy Johnstone. On the Celtic left, the speed and strength of Bobby Lennox was matched by the lion hearted Davy Wilson for Rangers.

Contested with as much commitment in the last minute as the first, the match ended as a two all draw, both sides having scored again in the second half. Undefeated, Rangers and their fans held their heads high, justifiably proud of their contribution to a magnificent showpiece. The Celtic support, drenched to the skin, hailed their heros, champions yet again.

Our neutral observer, sated on the quality of the football and drained by the emotional atmosphere, now knew that Rangers versus Celtic is the greatest club game in the world.

CHAPTER SEVEN

There was rare feeling of cameraderie in the steamy atmosphere in the Springfield that Saturday night, good will abounded, Rangers and Celtic supporters mingled happily, united in their common commitment to excel in their respective European finals.

In the corner occupied by Joe and the boys however, the celebrations were muted. While others about them talked excitedly about travelling to Lisbon, the lads had reluctantly come to terms with reality. The increased cost of the trip was beyond the means of them all except the unmarried O'Briens. The twins, however, had loyally decided that if the others were unable to go they too would stay at home. Joe it was who had made the decision to call off the trip all the more galling for him in that he had only just converted Betty, albeit reluctantly, to his point of view. And there, but for the temporary disappearance of Dunky McLinder's shaving brush, the matter would have rested.

On the following Saturday night when the regulars were again assembled in their favourite nook, they were joined by Dunky. Although no stranger to the Springfield, Dunky was not numbered among the Spring's regular customers. Unlike Joe and the lads who were happier in their "ain pub" surrounded by familiar faces, Dunky would flit happily from pub to club, his breezy open personality assuring him of an equally warm welcome in Hibernian Hall, Masonic Lodge, hotel lounge or homely howf.

"Ah heard you lads wis thinkin' about goin' to Lisbon," said Dunky, making himself comfortable in their midst. "Aye, that's right" said Paul rancorously, "We was!" "If ye're still interested," said Dunky, "Ah might be able to help ye." The lads exchanged sceptical glances, Dunky's reputation as a joker was legendary. "Huv ye robbed a bank or somethin'? asked Bill. "Go on, whit's the catch?" said Joe anticipating some trite punch line. Dunky looked aggrieved. "Ah mean it," he said, "Ah can help ye." "Ye're no huvin' us on?" asked Desmond, suspicion deepening his scowl. As it turned out Dunky was definitely not "having them on".

As luck would have it a couple of days after he and Bella had spoken to Anne Marie, Dunky had visited his cousin Alan in the lock-up Alan used as a workshop. Naturally Dunky had told Alan about the lads' predicament.

Alan McLinder hadn't said anything at the time which was not surprising since he was twisted in a nigh impossible contortion attempting to replace some inaccessible but indispensable component to the nether parts of a car engine. Alan's workshop was in Cambuslang and here Alan was in heaven. Alan's conception of paradise in the hereafter was just such a cold concrete lock-up perfumed by petrol and diesel oil, surrounded by an endless succession of broken down cars and presided over by an internal combustible deity.

Alan had an inherent affinity with the mechanical complexities of motor car engines. No problem it would seem was beyond him, previously stubborn blocks of mute metal were persuaded into chattering animation by his mystical attentions. Had his talents manifested themselves in an accepted art form, Alan McLinder would have been hailed as a genius. As it was, like many such gifted folk before him, Alan scraped by, little aware of his true worth and totally lacking any business sense.

A slim gaunt faced thirty five year old with long dark hair, Alan, like his cousin Dunky, was officially unemployed. To see his lanky profile encased in dirty denim, emerging from the Labour Exchange on Thursday mornings would be to dismiss him as just another too lazy to seek work which was then readily available. That was far from being the case.

"Signing on" was an accepted lifestyle for a section of the community at that time. Small time entrepreneurs, window cleaners, painters and car mechanics among them, plied their trades free from the irritants of formal bookkeeping and the necessity of filling in tax returns. Some of them waxed fat on their illicit earnings, not so Alan. Forever underpricing his work, seeking and deriving only the satisfaction of the job well done, he made only a modest profit from his enterprise, sufficient to subsidise his interests in renovating old cars and collecting recordings by Country and Western singers.

Alan differed from the norm in other ways too. Difficult though it may be for sane and well adjusted folks to accept the fact, there are some people who have no interest in football whatsoever. Alan McLinder was just such a one. Even so, he would have had to have been blind and deaf not to have been aware of Celtic's forthcoming final. Acres of newsprint had already been devoted to the subject to satisfy the avid demands of the fans. Among the array of topics slanted to meet this demand, Alan's eye had been caught by an item about driving to the Portuguese capital.

Alan's imagination had been fired, unlike rational men who day dream of improbably contrived goals and famous victories won against the odds, Alan's fantasies featured valiant rally drivers intrepidly traversing gruelling distances on rough roads in toughened customised cars. Fortunately for Joe and the boys, Alan's eccentricity was to work to their advantage.

It had long been Alan's ambition to participate in an international car rally. For this reason the proposal by a section of the Celtic supporters' club to run a cavalcade of cars to Lisbon for the final had excited Alan's interest in the occasion as no amount of soccer rhetoric could have done.

By a fortuitous coincidence, Alan had a acquired a few months previously, in lieu of payment for some job or other, a rusting hulk, the remains of a Commer van.

Even when new, the Commer was an uninspiring vehicle. A squat minibus, four square and snub nosed, with accommodation for twelve close packed souls including the driver. Inside, the uncomfortable driver's seat could be shared by two others, behind that were three double seats and, separated from them by a narrow aisle, three single seats. Access to the rear was gained through a near side sliding door and from the two doors which comprised the back of the van. In keeping with the philosophy of the designers the controls and instrumentation were primitive and functional.

At first glance Alan's inherited representative of the marque was somewhat unprepossessing. Closer inspection only confirmed this view. The bumpers which had once been chrome plated were pitted with rust which was apparent on all parts of the bodywork which hadn't already fallen off. One of the back doors hung at a drunken angle and was secured to its fellow by a lavatory chain and a cumbersome rust covered padlock. Only one of the four hub caps remained which only highlighted the fact that there were three missing, the survivor naturally showed ample evidence of corrosion. In the spartan interior, the seats were scuffed and worn, one window wouldn't open, another wouldn't close, and the floor was bare metal where it wasn't bare rust.

Nor were things any better mechanically. The steering was unresponsive, the brakes unreliable to say the least and the electrics were potentially more combustible then the engine, which was, to use the technical expression, totally clapped out.

Needless to say, Alan was delighted with his acquisition. Working steadily since then, Alan had restored the van to a state of roadworthiness, installing a more sophisticated braking system than had been in the original and replacing the obsolete engine with a six cylinder job, delighting in the challenge to his ingenuity occasioned by this refinement.

Alan had been eager to try out his handywork under testing conditions, so when Dunky told him of the lads' thwarted plans, it had seemed to Alan that both parties could only benefit from a meeting to discuss their mutual aims.

"No kiddin'?" said Joe, after Dunky had put Alan's proposal to the boys. Assuring them that the offer was genuine, Dunky left having agreed they would all meet again at Alan's lock-up the following afternoon.

The lads excitedly discussed this change in their fortunes, a change which might not have occurred if Ronnie McLinder had not misplaced his father's shaving brush thereby causing Dunky to be with Bella when Anne Marie had told them about the Lisbon trip, and enabling Dunky subsequently to mention the matter to Alan. Small matters each in themselves but indispensable pieces in the jigsaw of fate.

CHAPER EIGHT

The lads therefore were in fine fettle on the following afternoon when they set off towards Cambuslang, there to rendezvous with Dunky at his cousin's lock-up. It was a distance of little more than a mile and the boys capered and joked, elated by the Spring sunshine and their improved fortunes.

Dunky had given them directions, nevertheless they took some time locating the ramshackle structure situated at the end of a muddy lane in the lee of the sprawling Hoover factory. Even so the lads were still optimistic despite the unprepossessing appearance of the premises and the depressing heaps of rusting debris piled in the yard.

"There yis ur" said Dunky, opening a side door and beckoning them in, "Ah thought yis wur never comin'." "Sorry," said Joe, "We got lost."

Coming out of the spring sunlight it took the lads a moment or two to adjust to the gloomy interior of the workshop and the unpleasant posthumous reek of burned out pistons and punctured sumps, unfamiliar unsettling smells. Alan, who had a nodding acquaintance with most of the lads, greeted them shyly with the reserve of a performer needing the acclaim of his audience to assure himself of his own identity.

Wasting little time in conventional banalities, both parties being eager to get down to business, the cousins McLinder stood aside and ushered the lads into the dimness behind them. With a fine sense of the dramatic, Alan, waited until they were well positioned then, with a flourish, he tugged on an oil stained string and before them in a white flash of fluorescence was revealed the reconditioned Commer. Joe and the boys were aghast. Alan, to be sure, had spent many loving hours on the restoration of its working parts, but Alan, the pure mechanic, had done nothing to improve the van's appearance. What matter to him that the bodywork was dented and rotting, the doors still awry, the paintwork scratched and peeling and the brightwork blighted with rust. Like beauty, Alan considered such petty considerations to be purely superficial.

The lads shuffled uncomfortably, hopes that had been so high were once again dashed. Moreover they were in an awkward situation. By the smirk of bashful modesty on Alan's face, he was clearly expecting their enthusiastic approval and Dunky appeared not to be perturbed by the decrepit state of the vehicle. Obviously a large measure of tact and diplomacy would be required if offence was to be avoided.

"Well?" said Dunky, fair pleased with himself, "What d'yis think?" No one answered for a moment or two then Joe, hoping to set a diplomatic example spoke. "It's no' exactly whit we wur expectin'," he said. "What d'ye mean?" said Dunky aware for the first time of the lad's disquiet. "Ye wouldnae get the length o' Brigton Cross in that wreck," spouted Barney, the essence of tact. Alan was hurt, "whit's wrong wi' it?" he asked. Again the silence, the hesitancy, the unwillingness to offend but, since some explanation was necessary, Bill O'Brien took the bull by the horns "Look at it," he said, "It's fallin' tae bits." That did it, the floodgates were opened, the lads burst forth with a torrent of criticism, a catalogue of all the apparent defects and more than a few imagined faults. The Commer was crushingly and comprehensively condemned.

Another awkward pause followed. Alan was shattered and the lads, ashamed of their ruthlessness, were embarrassed. Only Dunky retained a clear perspective unaffected by the strained atmosphere. "Fair enough," he shrugged, "But apart from that it's perfect." His delivery and his timing were immaculate. The tension, which had been mounting, dissolved in the instant, laughter lightened the moment. Shrewdly then, Dunky capitalised on the change of mood. "Tell ye what," he said "why no' try it oot? Then see whit ye think." "Dis it go?" asked Desmond doubtfully. "Dis it go?" exclaimed Alan incredulous that anyone could doubt his ability, and eager to demonstrate his handiwork, "C'mon an' ah'll gie yis a hurl in it." The lads, not at all keen, looked to Joe. "Ach, why no?" said Joe, "Whit huv we got to lose?" "Only wur lifes," muttered Desmond nervously eyeing the van. And it was Desmond who was last to board the

34

Commer, his reservations increased by the vrooming engine which Alan was reving noisily in the enclosed space. Dunky opened the garage doors and they set off.

Alan was now in his element, his passengers were left bemused as he enthusiastically detailed the improvements he had implemented with a welter of technical jargon, incomprehensible for the most part, but from which they gathered that not only had he installed a new and more powerful engine, he had substantially and ingeniously altered the steering and the suspension.

As they drove through Cambuslang, the smoothness of the ride surprised the lads who had been perched apprehensively on the edge of their seats. By the time the van had started on the steep incline of Greenlees Road the boys were beginning to relax. Effortlessly the Commer glided up the testing slope and accelerated towards the East Kilbride Road. Once out in the open, Alan put it through its paces, sixty, seventy, eighty miles per hour with barely a tremor. Spanking new cars with shining chrome were left standing. "Wid ye look at that," enthused Paul Haddow "That wis a new Humber, they cost near eight hundred quid." The Hillman was passed with ease.

Skilfully double de-clutching Alan swung off Whirlies Roundabout and raced towards Blantyre. "Ur ye allowed tae go as fast as this?" asked Desmond, white knuckles gripping the seat in front. "We've no' got goin' get," replied Alan, relishing the experience. Going through Blantyre, Alan was given an opportunity to demonstrate the efficiency of the braking system when a myopic octogenarian, peering in vain through the steering wheel of a Morris Minor, came unexpectedly out of a side street. The Commer pulled up sharply, veering neither to the left or the right. Alan turned to his passengers, "Dual circuit brakes, servo assisted," he proudly explained. "Dual circuit eh?" breathed Bill impressed. The others nodded sagely as they picked themselves off the floor, not knowing what it implied but impressed nevertheless. By the time they arrived back at the lock-up the lads were lolling in their seats with proprietary ease. Alan's confidence in his improvements and alterations was vindicated.

Unsophisticated in such matters though they were, the boys now had every confidence in Alan and his van. All that remained to be done was for both parties to agree on conditions and terms. In this discussion, Alan, the brilliant engineer, was displaced by Alan, the inept businessman, as a result of which it took Joe and the boys all their time to persuade Alan to at least let them contribute to the cost of the petrol. Eventually when the financial arrangements had been settled, much to the advantage of the lads, there was still the delicate matter of the van's appearance. Determined to avoid any embarrassment caused by the thoughtlessness of the less sophisticated among the lads, Joe drew Alan aside and casually suggested ways in which the appearance of the van might be improved. Alan, who seemed to think it was the lads who were doing him a favour, duly noted Joe's suggestions and promised to see to them in the coming week.

The business thus settled to the satisfaction of all concerned, not least Dunky who had organised the meeting in the first place and had subsequently rescued it from collapse, the lads took their leave of the cousins and trooped off back to Rutherglen. Their step was as light as their hearts. Joe and the boys, the Springfield Regulars, were definitely on their way to Lisbon.

CHAPTER NINE

Sunday the twentyfirst of May 1967 was D-Day, D for departure.

The previous week had been a hectic time for all concerned. All the necessary preparations were attended to, mostly as a matter of course and mostly by the womenfolk.

Of all the essential preliminaries obtaining their passports was the most complicated and time consuming. Since none of the lads had been abroad before, (Desmond's honeymoon trip to the Isle of Man notwithstanding) this was the first time they had come across this particular bureaucratic hurdle. Eventually after much coming and going and form filling they acquired the necessary travel permits.

By Saturday all the arrangements were in hand and since they were not due to leave until the following morning the lads were delighted that they were free to attend the Junior Cup Final at Hampden.

The Scottish Junior Cup Final was then still one of the showpieces of the season, regularly attracting crowds of sixty or seventy thousand, played traditionally on the Saturday following the close of the Senior season and not as now on some indeterminate and entirely unsuitable Sunday afternoon to suit an uncaring and patronising television company. The event could be relied on to produce a thrilling hard fought game since the finalists were the successful survivors from over three hundred hopeful starters among the semi-professional clubs in the Country. A happy festive occasion when entire families and, even,

36

depending on the finalists, entire communities would turn out to cheer on their local heroes. The finalists in this instance were Kilsyth Rangers and, as luck would have it, Rutherglen Glencairn. So, naturally with their home town side involved, the lads were doubly keen to be there.

Consequently, on the Saturday afternoon among the hoard of Ruglonians wending their way up Curtis Avenue through King's Park to Hampden, were Desmond and Jean and their four kids, Paul and Anne-Marie, (whose mother had been persuaded to look after baby Kenneth), Barney and Bill and even old Mrs O'Brien. Joe was otherwise engaged, working for his living.

Sporting black and white favours, the Ruglonians gathered in the terraces at the King's Park end of the ground. Along with seventy thousand others they saw an exciting but drawn final, marred by the wet and windy conditions, typical of that damp Spring.

Nor was the weather any better the next day. On a dull and overcast Sunday morning the Regulars and their families waited, shivering with cold and excitement, on the arrival of Alan and the Commer, arrangements having been made to leave from the Mercat Cross at eight o'clock.

Their garish green and white scarves brightened the drab morning. The twins, perhaps fearful of being thought disloyal to the cause, wore in addition, Celtic jerseys and green white and yellow tammies. Desmond was surrounded by his wife and four children, the oldest boy petulantly kicking the steps of the monument, huffily angry at being left behind. Desmond was bent by the weight of a heavy and volumous tweed coat, his best suit and at least two visible jumpers. Jean was determined her man wouldn't catch cold in "thae furrin parts".

Joe and Betty stood a little from the others. Right to the last Betty had convinced herself that Joe would change his mind about the trip. She was now close to tears. Ever the self-dramatist, Betty was beginning to see herself as the heroine of a tragic parting. Truth to tell she was beginning to enjoy the situation.

Paul had arrived pushing the pram with baby Kenneth suitably attired in Celtic's colours. Unfortunately, his woollen tammy which proclaimed his allegiance also obscured his features. Anne-Marie further brightened the morning as far as the boys were concerned by wearing a green mini-skirt which was short even by her standards. On the pretext of looking out for the van the O'Brien boys had strategically positioned themselves so that Anne Marie was in their line of vision as she constantly fussed over her son. Mrs O'Brien had also noticed the short skirt and clucked her disapproval.

Anxiously the ever fretful Jean reproached her husband, "Ah thought ye said ye wur leavin' at eight o'clock?" she said. "The weans ur gettin' cold staunin' aboot." Equally anxious, Desmond squinted into the distance willing Alan to appear. "Here he is," called Bill O'Brien.

Alan drove past on the far side of the road, waving cheerily, then executed a U-turn and drew up by the ancient monument. It was now impossible to see the driver as the front seat was piled high with spare parts and tools including no fewer than four spare wheels. Alan was taking no chances, every contingency had been covered leaving only sufficient room for the driver to operate the controls.

The womenfolk, seeing the van for the first time, were appalled. On the face of it their concern was fully justified. Among the improvements Joe had tactfully suggested to Alan was that the van might benefit from a coat of paint. Being a logical sort of chap himself Joe had naturally assumed that Alan might have stuck to one colour, preferably matching the original which, admittedly was a faded travesty of its former glory. Alan, however, to whom equally logically, paint was paint, had started his patchwork job on the ancient blue of the exterior using a particularly bright pillar box red which had been the first pot to come to hand, generously applied with a whitewash brush. Exhausting this source and thinking to please the lads, Alan had subsequently finished it off in emerald green. The multi-coloured mini-bus had been improved in other ways. The back doors were now securely welded to a crossmember which, though inelegant, assured them against opening accidentally or otherwise. The window which wouldn't close was now boared over with newly painted hardboard. Despite, or more probably because of these improvements, the Commer looked even less presentable than it had the previous week.

"Ye're no' goin' in that?" Mrs O'Brien exclaimed in horror. Jean's natural agitation increased tenfold, Betty blushed, angry at being involved in this public humiliation and even Anne-Marie looked concerned. "Ah know it disnae look much," said Paul earnestly, "But it goes like a bomb." Joe had to step in quickly to deny the women the obvious retort. "Tell them aboot the improvements ye've made Alan," he said.

This was a masterstroke, while Alan bamboozled the women with unintelligible technical details, the lads tooks the opportunity to pack their bags into the van and stack them under the seats. Though little understanding what Alan had said the women were sufficiently convinced by his confidence and obvious competance to a reluctant acceptance of the situation.

Alan was now eager to get the trip under way. "Ur yis aboot ready?" he called to the lads. The enthusiastic chorus of confirmation was followed by loud sobs from Betty. The immaculate timing of her outburst had the desired effect, making her the centre of attention. Using a tiny cotton handkerchief wrapped decorously round her index finger, Betty daintily dabbed her damp eyes. It was an Oscar worthy performance. There were sufficient tears for tragic effect, but miraculously not so many as would upset her carefully applied make-up.

Tears were now the order of the day. Jean, Anne-Marie and Mrs O'Brien wept as they bade their men goodbye. Desmond's offspring snuffled too but that may have been due as much to the chill morning as it was to emotion and baby Kenneth, not content with tears, bawled fit to wake those Ruglonians enjoying their Sunday lie in.

The farewells promised to be a protracted business until Alan with finely judged sensitivity, interrupted them. "C'mon if ye're comin'." he called, "We've no' got all day." The lads clambered aboard, passers-by joined the families and by the time everyone was seated and Alan had started the van, the pavement was crowded with well-wishers excited by their enterprise and no doubt, to judge from the outward appearance of their transport, impressed by their temerity. "C'mon Celtic!" and "Bring back the Cup" they called. Inside the van the lads, spirits high as they took off on the road to Lisbon, broke into song:

"Sure it's grand old team to play for
Yes it's a grand old team we know
And if you know their history
It's enough to make your heart go Oh! Oh! Oh!
We don't care what the others may say
What the hell do we care
We only know that there's gonna be a show
And the Glasgow Celtic will be there."

CHAPTER TEN

Alan settled behind the wheel thrilled to be realising the ambition of a lifetime. The pile of spares on the seat beside him were testimony to the thoroughness of his preparations. On the dash in front of him were detailed route maps, ferry time tables and weather forecasts. Mechanically, geographically and even meteorologically every foreseeable complication seemed to have been covered. And yet there are eventualities which no amount of forward planning, however thorough, could anticipate.

From Rutherglen to Lisbon is a distance of 1,750 miles, there were still 1,749 miles to go when just such an eventuality occurred.

On the road from Rutherglen to Cambuslang there is a small complicated roundabout. Alan negotiated it with care and was about to accelerate when a figure darted out from one of the doorways of the Richmond Park Laundry and into the path of the van. Fortunately for Dunky McLinden, Alan was able to stop in time.

"Whit d'ye think ye're doing?" yelled Alan as his cousin opened the side door and swung aboard. "Ah've decided to come wi' ye," announced Dunky, closed the door and settled easily in one of the single seats. Taking the stunned silence for acquiescence, he stuffed a brown paper bag, containing a change of shirt and socks, under the seat.

"Just like that, ye're comin' tae Lisbon?" asked Barney, admiration mingled with incredulity. "Ye're no serious, ur ye?" said Bill. Their questions were obviously superfluous since who would go to all the trouble of packing a brown paper bag if he wasn't serious? "Aye, straight up," said Dunky, "An, how no? Ah might no' get another chance tae see the world." "Whit about Bella?" asked Desmond. "Ah'll get plenty mair chances to see Bella." replied Dunky.

The long and short of it was that on the previous day Dunky had enjoyed a particularly successful afternoon at the expense of William Hill (not of course that Mr Hill would have noticed). Even so the decision to join the Regulars on their pilgrimage had only been taken at the last minute. Impetuous as he was however, Dunky was sufficiently aware that such an epic journey required careful preparation. He therefore devoted almost five minutes to packing a bag, then generously stuffed the "Present from Portobello" jug with a fair proportion of his winnings before tip-toeing out of the flat. Half an hour later he had disturbed the Sunday morning peace at his brother's home close to the Richmond Park Laundry. Shortly after he was unceremoniously and physically evicted by his still semi-somnolent sibling and had then lain in wait for the van at the roundabout and, as he cheerfully concluded, here he was.

Alan was embarrassed. "Whit d'ye think lads?" he asked. "It's a' right by me," said Paul. "Aye why no? The more the merrier," said Barney. The concensus appeared to be in Dunky's favour although Joe hesitated. "If it's a matter o' money, don't worry, Ah'll pay ma whack nae bother," Dunky assured them. "It's no' that" said Joe, "Ah've nae objections tae ye comin' but as ye said yersell, ye only decided to come this morning'." "Whit's wrong wi' that?" asked Barney. Paul could see what Joe was driving at, "He'll no huv a passport," he said. "Exactly," said Joe.

For a moment Dunky looked crestfallen then, with dramatic elan, as a magician pulls a rabbit from his hat, he triumphantly produced a passport from his jacket pocket. "Ah didnae know you had a passport," said Alan astounded. The lads relaxed, all except Joe who knew Dunky of old. Calmly he called his bluff, "A' right Dunky", said Joe, "So ye've got a passport, but whose passport is it?" Dunky laughed, then casually replied. "It's ma brother's, he's no' usin' it this week." Uproar ensued. "But ye canny use that, it'll huv his photy on it," said Desmond. "Thae passport photographs ur a' the same," retorted Dunky, "They make everyone look like blood starved werewolves." Desmond begged to differ. "Jean thought mine wis a good likeness," he said. "Aye" said Dunky, "That's whit Ah mean." To his credit Desmond laughed with the others.

"Look at it this way Joe," said Paul, "If Dunky comes it'll give us an extra driver." This was certainly a consideration since apart from Alan only Paul was able to drive. Still Joe prevaricated but it was evident he was in a minority of one. "Ah wish ye'd make up yer mind," said Alan, impatient to continue the journey. Joe came reluctantly to a decision. "Well a'right, ye can come wi' us, but if ye huv any trouble wi' the Customs ye're on yer own. OK?"

That was "OK" by Dunky who sprawled in his seat in lordly fashion. "Carry on McDuff," he imperiously commanded his cousin, who dutifully did just that.

After the excitement of the departure the company settled down to the tedium of the journey. Leaving Glasgow behind them when they had passed the less than imposing entrance to Calderpark Zoo, the Commer headed south on the A78. It should be borne in mind that this was before we were blessed with the vast network of motorways and by-passes which, even allowing for the ever present repair gangs and inhibiting contraflow systems, make travelling so much easier but which we, crass and pampered, now take for granted. Alan's objective was to reach Dover by the end of the first day. It was a daunting prospect.

The Regulars settled as comfortably as they could in the crude, roughly upolstered seats. Joe demonstrated his organisational prowess early on by instituting a rota system whereby the lads each took turns on the marginally more comfortable double seats. That and other minor ground rules for the journey established, the lads relaxed, relatively speaking.

Since it was the Sabbath Day the Regulars passed the morning in the traditional Scottish way, reading the word as it was written in the "Post" and the "Mail", those twin journalistic pillars of the Scots' weekend. One brash and sensational, the other quaint and staid, and both aggressively patriotic, the "Post " the more intellectual of the pair, it being the one which features "Our Wullie" and "The Broons".

Alan made good headway during the morning and lunch was taken at a transport cafe at Scotch Corner and just before they joined the A1, the main route to the south. Only too well aware that their money, like themselves, had a long way to go, they feasted modestly on egg and chips. The twins indulged themselves to the extent of each having in addition a portion of beans, earning them disapproving looks from Joe and indelicate and entirely unoriginal comments from Dunky.

And it was at Scotch Corner that the Commer was dignified with a name of its own. Coming across country on the A66 there had been a stretch of road which had been newly resurfaced. Driving through the still wet tar at speed the van had been liberally splattered. The tar had imbeded itself in the many indentations and cracks on the Commer's rough bodywork. On their way back to the van after lunch Dunky noticed this and called to his cousin "Hey look at that Alan," he said, "Now ye've got a tar spangled banger.' And like the tar, the name stuck.

Late in the afternoon they stopped in the outskirts of Birmingham to give Alan a breather. Alan's notion of a breather was to stretch himself full length along the aisle in the rear of the van where he immediately fell asleep.

In marked contrast to the spartan interior of the van, the bare metal floor was now covered by a floral patterned carpet of the best quality. This had thoughtfully been provided by Alan's current girl friend, Gloria.

Alan was one of those most fortunate of men to whom women will give their all asking nothing in return. Never then feeling the need to marry and settle down, Alan's welfare was looked after by a succession of lady friends, happy to indulge what might be called their motherly instincts, were it not for the incestuous connotations. Gloria had been on the scene for some months now, a busty blonde, oversexed divorcee of independent means who had her own bungalow in Eastfield. Happy, generous and determined never to marry again, Gloria needed only a majority shareholding in a brewery to attain proverbial perfection.

As Alan lay down on the carpet he smiled to himself remembering the night it had been fitted. It wasn't only the carpet that had been laid that night.

Joe and the boys, with little option it might be said, took this opportunity to stretch their legs. Attracted by the sound of a ball being kicked on a nearby playing field, they came across half a dozen local lads lackadaisically passing the ball among themselves. A careless pass by one of them was intercepted by Bill O'Brien who flicked it into the air and juggled it from foot to foot before passing it back to the youths. In no time at all jackets had been placed for goal posts and an impromptu England versus Scotland match was under way.

About half an hour later Alan, refreshed by his catnap, tooted the horn to summon the lads back to the van. Conveniently the score at that time was tied at eight all. Both sides having enjoyed the encounter the Brummies accompanied the Regulars back to the Commer wishing them well for the rest of the journey and pledging their support for Celtic in the final.

"It just goes to show," said Joe as the van drove off leaving their new found friends behind, "The English ur no' sa bad efter a'." Desmond agreed, "Aye, a nice crowd o' fellas," he said, "But affy poor speakers. Ah couldnae make oot the hauf o' whit they wur sayin'."

On the last stage of the first day, Dunky entertained the company as they had hoped he would. To begin with he conducted a hilarious version of "University Challenge" based on the quiz in the "Sunday Post". After this, simply by affecting comic voices and quoting from the more ludicrous examples from the readers' letters page, he had the lads in stitches. Agony columns and horoscopes in the "Mail" were given the same irreverant treatment. Consequently when the Banger arrived at Dover the lads were in high spirits.

At the docks at Dover they were delighted to find several other groups of supporters en route to Lisbon. With the aplomb of seasoned travellers, experiences were compared and advice given. As a result of these conversations it was decided to spend the night on this side of the channel and cross on the ferry at 5.30 on the Monday morning.

The lads, much in need of ablution, took advantage of the facilities at the terminal, then, with the minimum of horseplay they settled down for the night in the spacious waiting room and following Alan's example they were soon asleep. So ended the first day on the road to Lisbon.

CHAPTER ELEVEN

Soon after five o'clock on the Monday morning the Regulars, refreshed by their night's sleep and a further session in the washroom, boarded the cross channel ferry. Even at that early hour there was an atmosphere of cordial bonhomie between the large contingent of Celtic fans, which had been swelled overnight by late arrivals and the regular long distance drivers. The shipping company, entering into the spirit of the occasion had had the ferry decked out in green and white bunting.

When the ferry sailed the lads were gathered at the stern. Shivering they gazed in awe at the famous white cliffs. Seen through the thin chilling mist on that May morning the vast parapet of chalk was an inspiring sight. A familiar view seen often enough from the stalls at the Odeon, but this they realised with a stomach turning thrill of excitement was the real thing. The unfamiliar sea smells, the salt air and the sickening hot stench of the ferry's diesel emissions, not to mention the danger of sustaining a direct hit from the hoards of seagulls overhead, brought home to them the stunning realisation of the magnitude of their undertaking. Even Dunky was reverently silent as they watched the cliffs recede into the distance.

The lads then ventured below deck. On Joe's advice they changed some of their currency into French francs then, marvelling at the prices, they laid in a supply of cigarettes and spirits against the rigours ahead. They were laden thus when they were joyfully accosted by a group of supporters they had met the night before who advised the lads to hurry to the ship's cafeteria where gigantic portions were being dispensed to Celtic fans. It so happened that the lad in charge hailed from Easterhouse. Generously he had taken it on himself to see that his fellow countrymen arrived on alien shores replete with what would be the last civilised breakfast they could expect until their return journey.

Soon after, as the ferry sailed into the harbour at Calais, the Regulars were reassembled in the Commer to disembark. Joe felt like the condemned man who had enjoyed a hearty breakfast. The moment he had dreaded since Dunky had joined them was imminent. Although at the time he had meant what he said about Dunky being on his own if there were complications at the Customs, now that there was a danger of that eventuality occurring, he was unable to summon up the resolve which had come so easily the previous day. He also realised there was another dimension to his dilemma. Should things go as he feared they would, the entire company would be implicated by association at least. Suppressing visions of the party being dragged in chains and slung into a stinking foreign prison Joe braced himself for the ordeal.

Dunky however, the cause of Joe's distress, was supremely unconcerned. The others too, after examining the passport, had tended to side with Dunky. As Desmond had cogently put it, "If Ah didnae already know you, an' Ah didnae know it wisnae you, Ah wouldnae huv knew it wisnae you." But like Joe, now that the moment of truth had arrived, they too had their reservations.

As the Banger trundled on to the quay, the tension inside grew. Hope sprung in their hearts when two car loads of fans were waved perfunctorily through but their hopes were dashed a moment later. The world weary Customs' official, blinking in affected amazement, halted their progress. Then, hands clasped behind his back, his face dark with suspicion and menace, he slowly circled the Commer. Arriving at the door beside Alan he stepped back a pace of two, then stood for a full minute shaking his head in disbelief. Fear gripped the hearts of the Regulars. The fear was intensified when, with a guttural Gallic grunt the guard summoned two of his colleagues. For what seemed like an age the three guards surveyed the rust ridden van. Eventually, with measured tread, the official approached Alan. One eyebrow, raised almost to the level of his uniform cap he uttered one word. "Lisbon?" Nervously Alan nodded in affirmation. The officer turned to his companions then, with a dismissive shrug which conveyed the message that he had now seen everything, he said "Lisbon!". Then all three burst into hearty laughter.

Inside the van the passengers exchanged anxious glances. The realisation that the natives were being friendly dawned gradually, uncertainly at first then with growing hysteria the lads joined in the laughter. Then, miracle of miracles, without further ado the officer stamped the passports and handed them back to Alan. "Lisbon," he said once more and this time there was a hint of admiration in his voice. The Banger was waved through, the official saluted their enterprise, "Bon Chance," he called after them.

It was only as they were driving through Calais that the lads realised how tense they had been. "Jings," breathed Barney, "That wis jist like one o' thae prisoner o' war filums." Airily Dunky trumpeted his vindication, "What did Ah tell yis," he said, "Nae problem." Safe now the Regulars were only too willing to agree with him. Noisily they claimed a retrospective bravado which had not been conspicuous during the crisis.

So much had already happened since leaving Dover it was hard for the lads to realise that it was not yet eight o'clock on a Monday morning, incident enough for a month of Sundays. It came therefore as no great surprise when the Banger sustained its first setback. Alan blamed it on the illogical French habit of driving on the wrong side of the road. Seven hundred and fifty trouble free miles there had been between Glasgow and Dover and now, after barely five miles on the continent, the engine rebelled, coughing and spluttering to a halt outside an unpicturesque village.

As Alan confidently set to repair the damage the Regulars went off to explore the hamlet. All the houses had wooden shutters and for the first time they noticed the indigenous aversion to paint. Even in the bright light of the May morning the buildings looked dingy with naked woodwork and whitewashed walls cracked and scruffy. Amid these unimposing homes they came across the French equivalent of a "Jenny-a'-Thing".

The store lacked the vitality of Ali's in Stonelaw Road and the lads had already passed it when Desmond called on them to wait and disappeared inside. A few minutes later he reappeared. His companions were shocked by his appearance, and his continual backward glances over his shoulder gave them cause for the utmost alarm. "Whit's up Desmond?" asked Paul. Dumbfounded, Desmond could only gasp and point to the shop. Joe, already shaken by the events of the morning, was gripped by the chill of dread. Nearing desperation he pleaded, "C'mon wee man, tell us whit's wrang". Desmond, pale and shaken, pointed to the store. "Ah canny believe it," he said, "They've no' got the "Daily Record"." The Regulars laughed, as much with relief as at Desmond's consternation. "Ye should huv taken the "Express" said Dunky. The laughter increased when Desmond replied in all seriousness that he would have but that they didn't even have that.

They were still laughing when Alan arrived with the van. Alan was keen to explain the intricacies of the repair. Joe and Paul, who were aware how important this was to him, feigned interest. They were just about to continue with their journey when Dunky dived into the village store only to reappear moments later looking much as Desmond had looked when he had come out of the shop. There was obviously something seriously amiss to affect Dunky so, the Regulars waited breathlessly for his explanation. "They've never heard O' Irn Bru," said Dunky incredulously, "Whit sort o' place is this?"

Only an incident of earth shattering proportions would have made any further impression on the Rutherglen contingent after such an eventful morning. Thankfully no such incident occurred.

Progress was steady throughout the day. During the morning they blithely passed signposts bearing the doomladen names of Arras, Cambrai, Armentieres, et al, blissfully unaware of their dire association for a previous generation.

Paris was passed by noon and in the evening they stopped for the night in the industrial town of Tours. Because of their limited funds hotels were out of the question so, putting into practice their experience from the night before, they drove to the main line Railway Station where they bunked down for the night. All except Alan, who slept like a babe in the Tar Spangled Banger.

CHAPTER TWELVE

On that same Monday evening back in Rutherglen Jean was fussing and fretting in the kitchen. The additional stress caused by Desmond's absence and the responsibility of looking after their four children single handed had Jean, if it was possible, in and even greater state of uncertainty than usual. She had dithered for a full five minutes unable to decide whether to open a tin of ham or a tin of corned beef for the evening meal, then committing herself to the corned beef had immediately wondered if the ham might not have been a better choice.

As far as her children were concerned, she had little cause for complaint. By the standards of their contemporaries the McNair kids were paragons of virtue and obedience. Jean of course knew this and, if she was honest with herself, would have admitted that she was using them as an excuse to cover her main anxiety. Strange to say it was worries about Desmond, or to be more specific, worries about Desmond's fidelity which were giving Jean most cause for concern.

A few nights before his departure, Desmond had been reading his evening paper when Jean had, hesitantly at first, brought up the subject of Betty Dolan. It was not in Jean's nature to speak ill of anyone least of all the wife of one of her husband's best friends. But there was about Betty something that stirred antipathy in even the least malicious, and there was no one less malicious than Jean — normally. Jean had started by recounting Betty's recent performance at Ann-Marie's house and had gone on to a more general criticism. Desmond had continued reading his paper, grunting noncommittally from time to time, more intent on Gair Henderson's sports' report in the "Evening Times" than in anything Jean had to say about Joe's wife. Eventually, Jean had come right out with it and admitted that she didn't really like Betty Dolan. Desmond had grunted at this point. "So you agree wi' me?" asked Jean. Addressed directly Desmond had been obliged to respond. "Agree?" he asked. "Aboot Betty Ah mean, whit d'ye think o' her?" Jean insisted. "Betty," said her husband, barely looking up, "Nice lookin' lassie," then as an afterthought, "Got a rare pair o' legs," he added.

It was typical of Jean that this remark, wrung reluctantly from her preoccupied spouse, should have sown the poisonous seeds of doubt. Even the insular Jean had heard of the phenomenon of the male menopause. Desmond's perfectly innocent remark had set alarm bells

48

clanging. If Desmond saw fit to comment on Betty's legs what unspoken thoughts did he harbour about Anne-Marie and her negligible skirts. Leaping from one conclusion to another in no time at all, in Jean's fevered imagination Desmond had become a promiscuous womaniser, flitting about the Continent sating his inflamed desires with a succession of voluptuous and compliant partners.

This then was what was troubling Jean McNair and on top of all this yet another decision was required of her. Whether to have peas or beans with the corned beef. Problems never come singly.

At about the same time Betty Dolan was wearily preparing her own meagre meal in her partially furnished palace in Croftfoot. Betty had had a hard day. She had been continually on the go at the insurance office where she worked as a secretary and her short lunch break had been spent on necessary shopping and to crown it all there had been a hold up with the trains.

The designation of secretary was, to be honest, an embellishment of the facts. It was an affectation which both amused and irritated her workmates in the typing pool. Haughtily ignoring their scorn, Betty persisted with her self-deception. After all didn't she work almost exclusively with Mr Henderson in Claims? There were naturally various snide remarks made about their constant collusion. Treating these comments with the contempt they deserved, Betty dutifully and to her credit, assiduously attended to Mr Henderson's correspondence. To his credit, Mr Henderson appreciated her efforts on his behalf and was flattered by her professional devotion.

Mr Henderson had been taken on by the company in his twenties, was now in his forties and would still be there in his sixties, acts of God notwithstanding. He was married, had two children and, most importantly as far as Betty was concerned, he lived in Clarkston. It was Betty's avowed intention to eventually make her home in that pleasant south side suburb. Before their marriage she and Joe had looked at houses in Clarkston but even the ambitious Betty had had to concede that the prices were more than they could reasonably afford, offers of over £2,000 being required. Instead they had contented themselves with the ingeniously, but contradictory termed, cottage flat which at £1,750 was within their means.

Sturdy four apartment family units, these cottage flats had been built for rental between the wars. They had at first sight the imposing appearance of large villas but on closer inspection were seen to be

49

divided into four flats, each with its own door and a share of the garden. Popular with young couples as a first home, surprisingly there were few takers when they were offered originally to the sitting tenants for the princely sum of £950.

As for her tardy return home Betty had good reason to be annoyed with herself. She had known when she arrived at Central Station that there was a disruption to the services on the Cathcart Circle and she could easily have gone for a bus from St Enoch Square. This option, unfortunately for Betty, was out of the question.

When she had first gone to stay in Croftfoot she had been happy enough to use the buses which were, if anything, more convenient and more frequent than the trains. The bus service however, had one overwhelming drawback which, to Betty's everlasting horror, she had not realised before her dignity, her selfesteem, indeed her entire social standing, had been dealt a severe blow.

Both bus services which went to Croftfoot from St Enoch, the 5 and the 14, had their ultimate destination in Castlemilk, a vast post war Corporation housing development which, in common with others of its kind, had acquired a unfortunate reputation as a consequence of the anti-social behaviour of some, but by no means all, of its inhabitants. Betty's distress had been caused by a colleague who had seen her board a bus and had assumed that, since the bus was bound for Castlemilk, so too was Betty. Betty was appalled at the very idea. Remembering the imagined humiliation was enough to bring her out in cold sweats. She had vowed there and then never again to allow herself to get into such an ambiguous situation, as a result of which it was now well known in her office that Betty Dolan would do nothing so common as to travel by bus. She, as she airily declared, commuted by train.

Betty piled her tea things in the sink then, thinking petulanty about Joe enjoying himself abroad, she left them unwashed, kicked off her shoes and lay out on the couch to watch television, revelling in her sloth.

Mrs O'Brien sighed and tipped into the bucket sufficient food to have sustained four Third World refugees or one fashion model for a month. Sadly she realised she would have to get used to the idea of cooking for one ageing widow. Sooner rather than later her boys would marry leaving her alone with her memories.

Memories of a marriage which from courtship to consumation, then

50

almost immediate separation, had covered barely one of her youthful years. Hugh O'Brien had been killed on active service in 1942, two days before Barney and Bill had been born. That had been the last of her youthful years. The struggle to rear her robust offspring in the cruel post war years had left its mark.

Myra O'Brien's generation were the last of the traditional subservient Catholic women, subordinated by the power of the priests, following in blind unquestioning faith the tenets of the Church, meekly accepting their poverty and ill health as God's will. Their bodies misshapen and wracked by constant childbearing, their lovemaking uninhibited only in the contraceptive sense, fearful of the wrath of the Church should they be thought guilty of avoiding their reproductive responsibilities.

Had Hugh O'Brien survived, there is nothing more certain than that with Myra's commitment to her maternal obligations, they would have substantially increased the O'Brien brood. As it was she had only her grandchildren to look forward to and, if her future daughters-in-law were anything like Betty Dolan and her kind, there would be precious few of them.

Mrs O'Brien sighed again, finished tidying the kitchen and prepared to go to evening mass.

In the Haddow home that Monday night Anne-Marie had impatiently coaxed baby Kenneth's feed into his tiny gurgling mouth. Though proud of her son and happy enough to parade him in the Main Street and show him off to her friends, Anne-Marie was less enthusiastic about the minutiae of motherhood. Hating the whole disgusting process she had bathed and changed her son by the time her baby-sister had arrived. Anne-Marie, reasoning that an equal amount of sauce was due to the gander, had decided to have a night out.

From this it might be supposed that Anne-Marie, mini-skirted flower child of the permissive society, was hell bent on a promiscuous orgy which shallow perceptions would have us believe were the norm in the swinging sixties. Far from it.

The sixties may well have swung in such places as Carnaby Street or San Francisco but in Rutherglen they sallied past in much the same way as any other era. Changes there were as ever there are, skirts were shorter, trousers wider, hair longer and colours brighter. Pop records, though not yet the travesty of music they were to become, were

51

increasingly dependent on electronic manipulations for novel effect, but mercifully less obtrusive since this was before the introduction of the obnoxious ghetto blaster.

The outward sights and sounds of the sixties were apparent in the Burgh as they were else where but, seek as you might, there was little sign of the drug taking and sexual licence associated with the times. There was extra-marital copulation to be sure but it was inspired as ever by love, lust, youthful indiscretion or plain old fashioned infidelity and owed nothing to fashionable decree.

Self-styled trendsetters may well have been turned on to psychodelic trips induced by the drug LSD. In Rutherglen in these pre-decimal days, LSD signified, not a mind bending experience but simply pounds, shillings and pence. The very idea of drugs was anathema to the average Ruglonian. In a spirited debate in the Springfield, self-hallucinatory drugs were ultimately pronounced to be an abomination, though at the start of the debate Auld Tam's patrons could pronounce self-hallucinatory only with difficulty and by the end, not at all, afterwards, staggering home in a glow of virtuous self-satisfaction induced by their moral rectitude.

The truth of the matter however was that Anne-Marie was going nowhere more decadent than the ladies' bingo night at the Glencairn Social Club.

And what of Big Bella? Had this domineering mountain of a woman nothing to say about her husband's apparent desertion? Had she enquired of his whereabouts among his acquaintances? Had she informed the Police? Had she even noticed his absence?

The answer to all of these questions concerning Dunky was "No". If she had given the matter more than a moment's thought she would, in normal circumstances, have realised something was afoot from the generous amount of money on the mantelpiece. Or if she had known how many pairs of socks her husband owned, she would have realised that he intended to be absent for some time since there were two pairs missing. In mitigation it might be pointed out that Dunky's disappearance on this occasion was unique in that there was a degree of premeditation involved. Even so, in a normal happy marriage, which despite their bombastic bickerings theirs was, it might reasonably be supposed that the unexplained absence of one spouse or the other might excite some comment from the deserted party. Bella however, could plead extenuating circumstances, she was not herself.

The same Bella McLinder whose mere presence intimidated strong men, silenced garrulous women and terrified impressionable children was, on that May night, a piteous cringing creature. The great bulwark of her immense frame had been breached by a Trojan horse. Big Bella had the toothache.

Bella was tormented, demented and obsessed by what Burns aptly described as the Devil's Disease. Torturously affected by cold or hot drinks alike, the incessant thrusts of pain undermined all her good intentions, impeded her movements, deprived her of sleep and dominated her consciousness, progressively weakened by every excrutiating blood boiling stab. Even in rare moments of respite, driven by a self destructive will to torment, her tongue gingerly prodded the puffy kernel of anguish, inflicting needless pain.

Toothache unfortunately, save in its grossest excesses, is an invisible affliction and the victim is thereby denied the comfort of unsolicited sympathy. To admit its presence results in, at best, a soothing expression of condolence instantly followed by a minutely detailed account of the sympathiser's entire dental history or, at worst, a blunt recommendation to visit the dentist.

This was what Big Bella feared most. Despite all evidence to the contrary she tried to persuade herself that the pain would go away, as it had come, without any outside intervention. In this Bella was being unrealistically optimistic, there was only one surefire cure and she knew it. One tentative approach to the Dentist's door had resulted in the malaise miraculously abating only to return subsequently with redoubled ferocity. Sooner or later the dentist would have to be consulted. Despite her suffering, Big Bella was determined it would be as late as possible.

CHAPTER THIRTEEN

"What d'ye call an Italian prostitute?" asked Dunky McLinder, ever eager to entertain. His fellow travellers groaned and tried to ignore him.

This was on the Tuesday afternoon. The Tar Spangled Banger was passing through the flat chalky fields approaching Bordeaux. The landscape, to use the term loosely, was dominated by seemingly endless rows of what the lads took to be gooseberry bushes. They would have been surprised to learn that these "gooseberry bushes" were in fact vines, the fruit of which would ultimately be turned into the famous wines of the district. The aspect was dull and uninteresting, the monotony of the scenery matching the mood of the Regulars.

Morale which had been high on Sunday and had been sustained by the exciting events on Monday was now at an all time low. The inevitable friction caused by their enforced proximity and the frustrations of the tedious endless miles had taken their toll. They were now well into the third day of their odyssey so it was hardly surprising that after three days close confined in that rusting hulk that minor irritations carelessly shrugged off in normal circumstances should, in the claustrophobic conditions, assume the importance of international issues.

The twins, mutual tolerance not being their strong point, were inclined to resort to fisticuffs to resolve differences of opinion, inevitably disturbing the peace and inflicting incidental injury on innocent members of the party. Paul, who had once aspired to be a drummer, beat an incessant tattoo on the back of his seat. Joe when he was bored, which was now most of the time, monotinously hummed the "Londonderry Air" in such a fashion as to render that most melodic of songs almost tuneless. Desmond sniffed with metronomic regularity, inflicting on the others a fiendish toture akin to that of a dripping tap. And Dunky told jokes . . . endlessly.

When Dunky had joined the company on Sunday morning, not least among the reasons the Regulars had had for welcoming his presence was his ability to enliven even the dullest party, his reputation as an entertaining companion was legend on his native heath. True to form, Dunky had consistently amused the company on Sunday and had cheered them on Monday. But such endless cheer can be wearing. There is no doubt that in small doses Dunky McLinder's presence would be welcome anywhere. Unfortunately, as the boys were rapidly learning, there is a point beyond which the joke wears thin. That point had been passed long since.

Undeterred by their sullen attitude Dunky tried again. "What d'ye call an Italian prostitute?" Alan was having an unaccustomed break from driving at the time and was adding to the angst in the van by lying in the central aisle, thereby inhibiting the already restricted movements of the others. Risking retribution from four adjacent pairs of boots, Alan took the bait. "A' right," he said, "What d'ye call and Italian prostitute?" 'A Naple tart," replied Dunky, punning the

Glaswegian pronounciation of Eve's favourite fruit with an approximation of the Italian place name.

Encouraged by the moans and groans which greeted this effort the comedian launched into yet another joke from a seemingly endless supply. "Did ye hear the one aboot the two fellahs paintin' the chapel ceiling?" No one said that they had, much good it would have done them in any case. Dunky went on "Billy and Jim were up on this scaffolding paintin' the roof inside the chapel when Jim's false teeth fell oot. He climbed doon tae get them an' when he came back Billy asked him if they were broken. "Naw" sez Jim, "the priest said ah wis dead lucky, he said they landed in the urinal." "Whit's a urinal?" asks Billy. Jim sticks his teeth back in his mooth, "How would ah know?" he sez, "Ah'm no' a Catholic"."

Despite themselves his audience laughed. Alan, perhaps out of loyalty to his cousin or perhaps because, apart from Dunky, he was the only other non-Catholic in the van, laughed loudest. Of the others only Desmond failed to register amusement but then it was generally agreed that he was more pious than most and may have taken offence at the sacriligious nature of the joke. Nevertheless, the tension inside the van was noticeably more relaxed for the next half hour at least.

It was Alan who was seated on the floor who first noticed that something was wrong. Joe, alerted by Alan's concern, became aware of it next. The rate of progress which Alan had maintained at a steady 60 mph whenever possible, 'A mile a minute,'' he explained, had dropped perceptibly. "Something wrong Paul?" Alan asked his co-driver. Paul cleared his throat and coughed an embarrassed cough, sounding alarm bells among the Regulars and bringing Alan anxiously to his feet. "Ah think we're lost,'' Paul reluctantly admitted. Alan was incensed. "Lost?" he bawled, "A' ye hud to do wis follow the road we wur on, we canny possibly be lost." "But we ur, so we ur," said Paul, miserable with guilt. Sure enough the road they were now on was much narrower and more winding than the long straight roads they had become accustomed to since arriving in France. Fortunately around the next bend they came across a small township. Sleepy, dusty and untidy as it was, at least there was a chance of finding someone who could help put them back on course.

"We'll huv to ask someone the way," said Bill. "Why no' ask that postie ower there," said Desmond pointing to a tall figure in official

55

uniform and sporting a pillbox cap with a braided skip. "That's no' a postie," said Barney scornfully, "That's the polis." Paul, relieved at being given an early opportunity to make amends, drew up alongside the gendarme.

The policeman was a tall thin man with limbs which seemed disproportionately long even for such a tall figure. The impression was of a collection of particularly long and slim French bread sticks arranged scarecrow fashion inside the officer's uniform. The notion was strengthened by his nose, a crusty torpedo of a nose, which protruded some way beyond the peak of his cap. The lawman regarded the Banger warily.

"C'mon then," said Alan impatiently to Paul who, having stopped the van made no attempt to communicate with the officer. "Whit's keepin' ye?" stormed Alan, "Ur ye no' gonny ask him the way?" "Ah canny speak French. Ask him yersel if your so smart," retorted Paul. For a moment the company pondered the predicament then, with the precision of a well trained chorus line, every head turned towards Joe. Resenting the responsibility but flattered by their confidence, Joe beckoned the gendarme who tentatively approached to within six yards then stopped, plainly reluctant to come closer. Joe didn't seem to be all that keen either as Alan flung open the side door and the others allowed him a free passage. Joe strove desperately to formulate a question in French while wondering in English just how he had got himself into this situation. His unease became more acute with the realisation that the others were following him.

If Joe was uneasy the representative of the French constabulary, confronted by six dishevelled and desperate looking characters, was terrified. His natural impulse was to turn and flee but manfully he held his ground, partly to uphold the dignity of his appointment but mostly, it must be conceded, because he was transfixed by fear.

Joe tried hard to think of something he could say in French — anything. At last, just when his companions were beginning to show some impatience, inspiration struck. "Skuzy m'wah," he addressed the gendarme, "Oo eh Leesbon?" Instantly the lads' apprehension changed to admiration. The Frenchman was less impressed but his fear diminished to be replaced by perplexity. He frowned but didn't answer Joe's query. Pleased with himself now that he had taken the plunge and reflecting that two years of French at school hadn't been wasted, Joe more confidently this time, and speaking much louder since he reckoned there was a better chance of being understood, tried again. "Oo eh Leesbon?" Then, as an afterthought, "Seal voo plate."

Seen from the gendarme's elevated point of view, the Regulars did indeed appear to be a bunch of desperados. Frantically the policeman, striving vainly to appear unperturbed, attempted to put the situation into some rational context. Unfortunately, speed of thought or action was not a prerequisite for his sinecure in this sleepy provincial hamlet which afforded him little opportunity to use his initiative. However, not for nothing was he an avid reader of Simenon's Maigret books. How, he wondered, would his hero handle this situation? Almost audibly his mind embarked on a process of elimination. Discarding the notion that they might have come from outer space he had just decided they were drug crazed Parisians when, as often happened to Inspector Maigret, all became clear. Of course "Le Football!" Now it all added up, the British van, the prominent display of club colours and "Leesbon". "Mais Oui" he thought, then smiling broadly, delighted by his brilliant deduction, he launched into a frenzied discourse in his native tongue, in the course of which he welcomed the visitors to his country, wished them well for the forthcoming Cup Final and gave them the directions they required. Unfortunately, so carried away was he by his feat of detection, his speech was delivered with such passion as to make it unintelligible even to his own countrymen. And, since it is impossible for an excited French provincial gendarme to speak unaccompanied by gross gesticulations, the previously silent and petrified sentinel of the peace was transformed into a verbose human windmill.

It was now the Regulars turn, in the face of such exuberance, to put up a brave front. Once more the boys looked to Joe since he was the linguist after all. Alan however came to Joe's rescue. Thrusting his map at the Frenchman he braved the whirling arms and with singleminded determination he extracted the information he required. Then as soon as he tactfully could he extracted himself from the gendarme's arms which, when not rotating like indisciplined propellers, seemed intent on embracing the reluctant Ruglonians. Alan leapt into the driving seat and fired the engine; in an undignified scramble the others dived into the van desperate to escape the long flailing arms of the French lawman.

Once safely inside the Commer, Joe felt it was only right to thank their benefactor and no doubt to demonstrate that the extent of his French vocabulary was far from exhausted. "Mercy bow coo," he said,

57

then just to gild the lilly since he too was a fan of Inspector Maigret, albeit only through the recent television series, "Mercy bow coo patron!" The Frenchman's eyes glistened with emotion, his arms stretched out towards the van he called out as the Banger took off, "Vive L'Ecosse!" Already the van was picking up speed but at last he had said something that Joe understood. Joe felt obliged to respond in kind. Just before they rounded the bend leaving the gendarme waving an energetic farewell with both hands, he called back, "Up the French!" Honour was satisfied.

Joe relaxed after his efforts, basking in the admiration of his colleagues, his already exalted position enchanced by the practical application of his bilingual prowess.

Desmond felt a bit sheepish. "Imagine me thinkin' he wis a postie an' here he wis a polis a' the time," he reflected. "Ah'd rather be a French polis than a French postie," said Dunky, "Ye wouldnae catch me walkin' aboot wi' bundles of French letters!" The extent to which the incident had restored the morale of the Regulars can be judged from the fact that they laughed at this rather obvious comment.

Once more headed in the right direction, the Commer sped towards the Spanish frontier. For the time being their good humour restored, the lads were back on speaking terms, that is to say mutual insults were exchanged. Under cover of the ribaldry Desmond tugged furtively at Joe's sleeve and whispered fiercely. "Hey Joe, what's a urinal?"

CHAPTER FOURTEEN

Big Bella arrived at the dentist at 5.15 on the Tuesday evening. The receptionist respectfully ushered her into the waiting room. The receptionist was a vain girl with hair piled high on her head in a wonderfully intricate series of coils. The heavy mascara on her eyelashes and the severity of her hairstyle ill-became her youthful features. Given a spark of intelligence or personality she would have been an attractive child.

This was Bella's second visit to the surgery that day. After another demented and sleepless night, Bella had reluctantly accepted the inevitable. Imagine her chagrin therefore, having overcome her fear, to be told by the receptionist that appointments were necessary at all times. Emergencies could be attended to first thing in the morning but, since it was now past the time set aside for such emergencies, the dentist would be unable to see her until the following morning at the earliest. This said, the receptionist busied herself with the more important task of filing her nails. Big Bella was incensed, she had no intention of spending another night in pain.

It should be explained lest it might be wondered why even such a young and inexperienced receptionist could have made such a basic misjudgement of character, that the girl had obviously received the same training in customer relations as is nowadays given to checkout girls in supermarkets. Sighing impatiently and staring steadfastly at a point above and beyond the recipient of her homily and accompanied by the obligatory bored and sullen expression the girl had imparted the information, as was her wont, in a flat monotonous tone with ill disguised contempt for someone who didn't already know what she knew so well, resenting the intrusion of this or any other patient, without whom she considered the job would have been perfect.

Under normal conditions Big Bella was quick tempered, suffering from the obsessive stress and agony of prolonged toothache, Bella was positively explosive. The receptionist, breaking the habit of her working life, looked directly at the prospective patient for the first time and quailed.

Credit must be given where credit is due, suffering intensely and provoked by the receptionist's high handed attitude, Big Bella might have been forgiven if she had followed her natural inclination and flattened the insensitive child.

Acting however with commendable restraint and, with a rare touch of diplomacy, Bella explained her predicament and tactfully suggested that perhaps if the girl tried very hard, some way might be found to accomodate her. This in essence was what Big Bella had to say. It would be indelicate and offensive to give a verbatim account peppered as it was with profanities and anatomical allegories. In addition the implicit threat of violence, made more chilling by the certainty of its execution, left the receptionist in no doubt as to what was expected of her.

Learning quickly, and in the interest of self-preservation, the foolhardy girl suddenly found to her surprise that there had been a cancellation at 5.30 and even although the dentist had a pressing engagement that evening, she would personally persuade him to fit Bella in.

By the time Big Bella arrived for her evening appointment so stiff was her face with poison from the abcess that, for the first time since her infancy she was unable to speak. Unfortunately for Dunky it was just his luck that this phenomena should have coincided with his absence. As far as the receptionist was concerned, there was no need for Bella to say anything. Bowing and scraping and careful not to turn her back on her, the girl respectfully ushered Bella into the waiting room, waited until Bella had compressed her massive frame into an ancient basket chair which creaked and groaned in protest, then beat a hasty retreat to safety behind her desk.

There were already two other patients in the waiting room; an unkempt grey haired woman in her fifties dressed in a shabby tweed coat more suited to a winter's day than mid May, even such a miserable May. A younger woman sat beside her, her smart outfit complimenting her red hair and pert good looks. The two women were in conversation although the younger one was monopolising the exchange when Bella entered. So great was Bella's pain and discomfort that it was some time before she became aware of what was being said.

Not noticeably reticent Bella normally would have relished the opportunity to voice her own forthright opinions on occasions like this. In fact, it is reasonable to assume that in normal circumstances she would have had a considerable amount to contribute, if only to put the young redhead in her place. The girl had immediately impressed Bella as being a "right stuck up wee bitch". Struck dumb with pain Bella could only listen with growing rage as the redhead prattled on in an irritating and affected accent. "Yer mooth's fu' o' jorries hen," thought Bella.

The redhead had been telling the older woman about her responsible position as a secretary in a city office. "A right wee puke," thought Bella. The voice grated on in this vein for some time explaining it was not normal practice to allow employees time off for dental appointments but, such was her standing with her boss, an exception had been made in her case. "He was probably that glad to get rid o' the puke for a while," thought Bella.

The older woman spoke for the first time since Bella had come in. "Here, ah hope ah'm no gonny be much longer, ma man'll be in fur his tea soon." the younger woman, irked slightly by the change of subject, quickly took up the reins again. "Lucky me! That's not one of my problems this week," she said, "My hubbie's away to Lisbon for to see the Celtic." Bella groaned inwardly, she might have known. If there was one thing worse in Bella's opinion than "a right wee puke", it was "a right wee Papist puke".

The redhead obviously expected the older woman to be impressed by this information and was visibly put out by her riposte. "That a fact?" said the older woman, "Ma man's flyin' oot on Thursday mornin'!" "Good fur you auld yin" thought Bella, "That's put her gas in a peep."

The younger woman rallied immediately. "Well of course Joe could have flown but he decided to make it a proper holiday," she drawled, "He's travelling wi' his chums in a luxury coach. Apart from the football they'll be doing the cultural thing of course." "Oh of course!" thought Bella murderously. "They'll probably stop off in Paris to visit the Loo," continued the redhead. "Aye, an' they'll probably stop off in Rome to visit the Pope," thought Bella whose knowledge of European geography was on a par with the redhead's pronounciation of the name of the Parisian art institution.

"Ah've tae get chops," said the older woman mournfully. The redhead tutted sympathetically, "Don't you worry about it," she cooed, "He'll give you a jag and you'll no' feel a thing." The grey haired woman squinted doubtfully at the redhead. "Ah've tae get chops for ma man's tea," she explained as though to a child, "An' if he . . ." she jerked her head towards the dentist's surgery, ". . . if he disnae get a move on the butchers'll be closed." The younger woman clapped her hands to her cheeks and screeched excruciatingly. "Oh silly me, how stupid!" she giggled, "Whatever must you think of me?" What wouldn't Bella have given to have been able to tell her.

As Bella was to remark later in the retelling of the experience, the temptation to "Draw ma haun across her jaw" was becoming irresistible when, fortunately for the redhead, the waiting room door opened and the receptionist, careful to keep a respectful distance from Bella, called "Betty Dolan." The redhead crossed to the door, halted for a moment and turned to the grey haired woman. "Well bysy-bye then, awfy nice talkin' to you," she said then, giggling stupidly again, "And I hope you enjoy your chops," gave one last nerve rending peal of laughter and was gone. The grey haired woman looked soulfully towards Bella who nodded sympathetically, two souls with but one thought: "Daft bitch!"

Bella sighed reflectively, the redhead's "hubbie" and his "chums" sounded like a right shower of chancers and Catholic chancers at that. Dunky might have his faults but, gratefully she thought, at least he didn't associate with people like that.

61

CHAPTER FIFTEEN

Dawn on the Wednesday morning found the Tar Spangled Banger sheltered from the bright May sunlight in a pine grove. The pine grove was situated off the main road some way south of the Basque town of San Sebastian. San Sebastian was on the way to Lisbon, the Banger was not. Come noon the Commer was still sheltered from the bright sunlight in the pine grove.

The unintentional long lie might have been caused by the accumulative effect of three hard days on the road or perhaps the comforting warmth of their first Spanish morning. It might even have been something they had eaten and some may have put it down to the local water. Then again, the cheap Spanish wine might just have had something to do with it. Whatever, the cause, for all the difference it made to the Springfield Regulars, Wednesday morning might never have been.

They had travelled further and for longer than they had intended on the previous night. Alan, competing in his imaginary rally, had set demanding schedules for the journey and, although the time lost when Paul was at the wheel had been negligible, Alan insisted that they should cross the Spanish border that evening.

No one argued with him, he was the navigator and he knew best. And besides, the lads had become tired of France. Not having grasped the principle of scale, they found it hard to understand why two days should be needed to get from the top to the bottom of page seventeen, (France), in Bill's old school atlas, when page four, (Scotland), and page three, (England), had, between them, taken only one day.

Although Joe experienced some anxious moments before they arrived at the border, thinking about Dunky's passport, or rather Dunky's brother's passport, none of the others appeared to be worried, least of all Dunky. Joe needn't have worried, the Customs Officers, as they had at Dover, waved them through, wishing them well. In the course of the day the Celtic cavalcade, the contingent of twenty odd vehicles travelling to Lisbon more or less in convoy, had passed this way, their cheerfulness and obvious devotion to their team had favourably impressed the border guards.

Leaving France behind them the Regulars started on the Spanish leg of the journey. Only Desmond was sorry to be out of France. From a professional point of view he would have been interested to see in what way the letters carried by French postmen differed from British letters. He made a mental note to keep his eyes peeled on the return trip.

It was fairly late in the evening when Alan finally pulled the van off the main road and into the pine grove. Glad to excercise their stiff limbs the Regulars tumbled out.

Although there was a well defined track leading to the grove, suggesting that it was probably a popular picnic area, it was only by chance that Alan had found this spot. And it was by chance that Paul found the pool. He fell into it, head first, fully clothed. The pool was only about thirty yards from the van, hidden from immediate view by a rocky rise. Paul had removed his glasses to wipe his weary eyes, slipped on a loose stone and toppled headlong into the water. The twins were first on the scene and, mistaking Paul's anguished cries for help, kicked off their shoes, held their noses, yelled "Geronimo!" and leapt into the water. Within minutes they were joined by Dunky, Alan and Joe. Only Desmond hesitated. "C'mon it's smashin'," called Bill. "But ah canny swim," said Desmond. "Me neither!" shrieked Paul, just before he went down for the third time. Joe called the others to Paul's assistance. Reluctantly the O'Briens and the McLinders abandoned a robust bout of water wrestling and hauled Paul, coughing and splutting to the shallows under the bank. There, propped on a submerged rock, he was left to recover as best he could while hostilities were resumed.

Released from the inhibiting restraints imposed on them in the confines of the van, the boys gave a free rein to their youthful exuberance, enjoying the freedom of movement, while incidentally, and equally importantly, washing away the accumulated grime of the trip.

Eventually, after much cajoling, threatening and, in the end, the employment of brute force, Desmond was persuaded to take the plunge. Wading at first in the shallow water beside Paul, he was dragged screaming to the centre of the pool where he was ducked, unceremoniously by the twins.

For half an hour the Regulars luxuriated in the water. On Joe's instructions they had removed their clothes and laundered them in primitive fashion. At last, refreshed but tired, they had emerged to the realisation that their clothes were sodden and there was little likelihood of them drying before morning. Fortunately, Mrs O'Brien had had sufficient foresight to pack an extra pair of jeans for each of the twins and their sweaters were still dry. Alan simply stepped into his one piece boiler suit. Dunky delved into his brown paper bag and hauled out a pair of crumpled corduroys and a wrinkled t-shirt. Joe, who had disappeared behind the trees, returned, to the astonishment of all, dressed like a band box, trim and neat in his best suit, collar and tie. Realising the incongruity of his outfit he bashfully explained that Betty had packed these things in case he "met someone important". When Joe appeared thus, Paul skipped into the van and, in a few moments, reappeared equally well dressed. Not that this was down to Anne Marie's foresight, his suit just happened to be first thing to come to hand when she was packing. Only the dripping dishevelled Desmond remained to be dressed. The only dry garments he had were a well worn Fair Isle pullover and his outsized overcoat. respectability was achieved when Barney produced a baggy pair of football pants.

The excercise had made them hungry, much as walking, talking and even just breathing made them hungry. Since their arrival on the Continent their main sustenance had been in the form of bread and cheese. The long sticks of French bread had reminded them of their schooldays when lunchtimes had been spent with their arms encased in similar loaves bought, against the wishes of their parents, from Galbraith's Stores. Apart from the bumper breakfast on board the ferry on Monday morning, they had had only one other conventional meal. But the astronomical cost which, after laborious calculations, they worked out to be over five shillings each, and the uncertainty about what they had actually eaten, put an end to that particular extravagance. It was then decided that in the interest of economy they would in future fend for themselves and, since they had no cooking facilities, fending for themselves meant bread and cheese, augmented by the occasional apple. Imagine the outcry there would have been at home had they been asked to survive on this staple fare. But of course, these were exceptional circumstances, this was a pilgrimage and if sacrifices were required they would be stoically borne.

And so on the Tuesday night the oddly attired Regulars sat down to their frugal meal and that was the start of their troubles. Like many a misadventure it seemed a good idea at the time. In fact, given more experience on the part of the participants, it was an excellent suggestion. Dunky suggested it first, although he subsequently denied it, blaming Alan. Whoever it was makes little difference since no one opposed the idea, on the contrary. There was an immediate and unanimous chorus of approval.

Dunky, (or was it Alan) on receiving his allocation of bread and cheese remarked on how dry it was and wished he had a pint of McEwan's heavy with which to wash it down. That did it. In no time at all, Joe and Paul, since they were the best dressed, had been despatched to collect a "Carry Oot" from the local equivalent of an off-licence in a nearby village.

On their return the others were crestfallen, but not as surprised as they might have been two days ago, to find that not only was there no McEwan's beer available, there was no beer at all worthy of the name to be had for love nor money. Wine there was however, gallons of it. After adjustment had been made from £ s d to francs and then into pesetas, Joe was surprised and delighted to find that a bottle of wine could be had for less than the price of a pint of beer.

It had already been agreed, for economic reasons, that their alcoholic consumption on the trip should be kept to a minimum, so Joe restricted the company to only two bottles each. Joe was later to justify his decision on the grounds that if the lads could consume upwards of six pints of heavy on a Saturday night, two bottles of insipid looking wine would be well within their capacity. This of course is the mistake they all made.

Having worked up a reasonable thirst in the course of the day the boys, without exception, downed their first bottle as they would a pint of their favourite beverage at home. Grimacing and spluttering they declared themselves glad not to have been born Spanish and have this as their normal tipple. However, halfway into their second bottle their attitude changed. "Here, this stuff's no' sae bad efter a'," said Paul. "Aye, it grows on ye," agreed Bill. Desmond wasn't so sure, "Ah'm a bit dizzy," he complained. "Tell us somethin' new," snorted Dunky.

Inspired by the alcohol now flowing freely through his veins, Dunky told some jokes. This, of course, was not unusual, what was unusual was that he told them while simultaneously doing a headstand and attempting to drink from the bottle whilst in an upsidedown position. Inevitably the cogency of his tales suffered, although you would never have known it from their reception. Even the silliest gag, in fact the sillier the better, provoked uproarious laughter among his tipsy friends.

The twins then attempted their Flannigan and Allan impersonation. It was, as you would imagine, a disaster. Their singing was bad enough normally but, deluded by the effects of the wine, they bawled out the melody obviously under the impression that what they lacked

65

in finesse could be compensated for in sheer volume. Allowances should perhaps be made for the undulating nature of the ground, even so their choroegraphy was erratic in the extreme. The famous synchronised steps, which were the trade mark of the old music hall act, were clearly outwith present capabilities. Consequently it was only a matter of time before the pair, legs entangled, toppled and sprawled in an undignified breathless heap accompanied by the raucous cheers of their colleagues.

This was followed by a rousing sing-along, thoroughly enjoyed by the participants, but surely a painful experience for any audience there might have been. The grand finale was provided by Desmond who, in his youth had been, although he said it himself, "a dab hand at the Irish dancin'". There was no doubt about his proficiency and in many ways his was the most accomplished performance of the evening. He was unfortunate therefore that his comparatively skilful interpretation of the traditional steps should have affected his friends in the way that it did.

At the best of times there is a comic aspect about Irish dancing wherein only the legs, but most importantly the feet, participate in intricate and complicated steps. The rest of the dancer's body remains rigidly upright and the arms are held in such a position as to make them appear much longer than they actually are. The overall impression is of a marionette whose operator had not yet mastered the intricacies of manipulating all the strings simultaneously.

So, not only did Desmond have to contend with the inherent absurdities of the dance, it has to be admitted that, had he deliberately set out to provoke hilarity, he could hardly have chosen a more appropriate outfit. Even in a stationary position he looked ridiculous in his worn Fair Isle pullover which clung tightly even to his puny chest. The borrowed football pants reached almost to his knees exposing his pale spindly legs, made to look even more skinny by his cumbersome boots and on top of all this he still wore his outsized overcoat.

All this was amusing to begin with but when Desmond launched into a complicated jig, humming the tune with increasing breathlessness through clenched teeth, the lads fell about laughing. Undeterred, Desmond persisted with his routine, his clog like boots stomping away at the ends of his matchstick legs and his overcoat, seeming to have a life of its own, jerking in eccentric counterpoint to his flashing feet. The Regulars were helpless, the tears ran down their cheeks. The solemnity with which Desmond performed, even when confronted by this philistine reaction, only made them laugh all the more. Eventually, his exhibition over, Desmond bowed the stiff conventioanl bow he had learned as a boy and keeled over.

The mood was now sublime. In an effort to sustain the euphoria, the supply of wine being exhausted, the Regulars recklessly set about the whisky they had bought on the ferry. The next thing any of them knew it was high noon on the following day. Insides heaving and heads throbbing they were shaken, prodded and kicked to a basic form of consciousness by the McLinder cousins.

Dunky had been the first to surface which may have been due to his unconventional constitution, accustomed as he was to irregular hours and impromtu binges, but most probably it was because he had consumed less wine than the others. In his attempt at upsidedown drinking most of the contents of his second bottle had gone into his ears or down his shirt front. Nevertheless, hardened campaigner that he was, the cheap wine had had a knockout effect. After a laborious and painful ten minutes he had battled to a kneeling position and crawled over to rouse his cousin.

Alan was sprawled grotesquely underneath the Banger. Unfortunately for Alan, Dunky didn't take this into account when he shook him awake. The sharp blow Alan received to his left temple when he suddenly sat up was probably the last thing you would have wished on your worst enemy wakened in similar circumstances. On the other hand, it may have helped to clear his befuddled brain.

The others were wakened in turn, dragged reluctantly from the morass of their drunken dreams to the head splitting reality of the glorious summer's day. Little was said, thought itself was a tiring physical imposition on their turgid minds, but the sentiment common to all, could be summed up in two words — "Never again".

Taxing their weary minds and bodies to the limit and accompanied by countless moans and groans the lads dragged themselves to the poolside, removed their clothes and wallowed in the cool water. The contrast to the previous evening's shenanigans could not have been greater. Where there had ben tomfoolery there was total inertia, where rollicking boistrous noises had reverberated in the pines the silence was broken only by the odd wail of lamentation or the sad sounds of retching. This was the morning after with a vengeance.

After a lengthy soak the Regulars gathered round the van. The therapeutic value of the pool had been a godsend, the dip had revived them to such an extent that some of them were able to walk, or if that's perhaps pitching it a bit high, some of them were able to traverse the short distance from pool to transport in an almost upright position.

By this time, Alan, who now had an interesting technicolour bruise above his left eye, had recovered sufficiently to realise that his schedules would have to be drastically revised to compensate for the lost morning. Clearly the first priority was to get the van on the move again but, equally clearly, he was in no fit state to drive at the moment. Fortunately, Dunky, demonstrating remarkable powers of recuperation, declared himself fit to drive. And so, only half a day late, the Springfield Regulars continued, albeit with the greatest circumspection on the part of the substitute driver, on their way to Lisbon.

CHAPTER SIXTEEN

"Ah'll bet they're fair enjoyin' themsel's just now," said Anne Marie, "Ah wish ah had half their luck." Anne Marie was complaining to Desmond's wife Jean. "Aye ah know whit ye mean," Jean sympathised, "It makes ye wish ye wur on holiday yersel! Ah'd love a chance tae lie back an relax for a wee while wi' nothin' tae worry aboot."

They were in Anne Marie's kitchen on the Wednesday afternoon, Jean had dropped in for the company as much as anything but found herself dressing baby Kenneth having already fed him, bathed him and changed his nappy. Anne Marie, none too keen on that aspect of parenthood, had become quite adept at exploiting the motherly instincts of her visitors. "Ye'd think we might have heard from them," moaned Anne Marie, "Aye, a postcard wid'nae huv gone wrong," agreed Jean, somewhat absentmindedly.

Jean was still obsessed with the notion of Desmond's infidelity. Photographs published in the Glasgow papers of Celtic fans arriving in Lisbon had shown supporters posing in groups accompanied by Portuguese beauties in national costume. This, of course, was nothing more than a public relations exercise, that the same group of local lovelies would also be seen in the Milanese journals with groups of Inter fans would never have occurred to Jean. Those dark haired voluptuous models with flashing eyes and jutting breasts served only to flesh out the fantasies with which she tortured herself.

Images of Desmond in a variety of compromising positions haunted her. Even now there flashed into her mind a picture of a nubile Portuguese maid, pouting with passion, her sensuous body straining with desire for Desmond who was provocatively undoing the buttons on his tweed coat to reveal that, apart from his tackity boots, his person was as unfettered and unadorned as the day he was born.

"Ah said, they'll probably say they wis too busy," said Anne Marie, and not for the first time. Overwhelmed by the sheer eroticism of her daydream Jean had failed to respond. "But ah dare say they'll find plenty o' time tae enjoy themsel's," concluded Anne Marie. "Aye, ye can say that again," rasped Jean and Anne Marie was surprised by the amount of bitterness in her voice.

Mrs O'Brien would have felt easier in her mind if she had heard from her boys but she at least was sufficiently realistic not to read into the situation more than there was. Philosophically she accepted that even if it seemed hurtful there was no harmful intent on the part of her sons, that was just the way they were.

In comparison to the others, Betty Dolan was fortunate indeed. That morning she had received a postcard from her husband, despatched, as she thought somewhat melodramatically, from somewhere in France. Some effort was required to decipher Joe's hastily scribbled handwriting but eventually, having done so, Betty was disappointed to find, not a profession of everlasting love, but the banal declaration: "Having a good time, see you soon. Love Joe." If the text was trite the picture on the card was uninspiring save in a historical context. Close inspection of the faded sepia print revealed women in ankle length dresses, men with winged collars and horsedrawn transport.

Perhaps if Betty had known of the frustrations and disappointments of the other women she might have been more appreciative of Joe's efforts. As it was, the card, which in all probability had been in the thick of and had survived two world wars, was torn to shreds and consigned to the rubbish bin within minutes of arriving at Croftfoot. So incensed was Betty that she decided on drastic action. When she returned home that evening she had in her bag a packet of chocolate biscuits.

The only other communication to reach the home front was received by Gloria, Alan's lady friend in Eastfield. Writing in pencil in a small cramped hand, Alan enthused in as much detail as space would allow, over the alterations he had made to the Commer and on their effectiveness. Gloria, as you might imagine, was less than excited by most of what her lover had to say but, squeezed into the last paragraph, there was one interesting piece of information.

Shortly after Gloria received her postcard she met May McLinder, Dunky's brother's wife, who in turn ran into Big Bella in the Main Street. May was a small thin woman in her thirties with a penchant for bright red lipsticks and matching nail polish which clashed harshly with her hair which, apart from half an inch at the roots, had been inexpertly bleached to a dull yellow. May wore a three quarter length imitation leopardskin coat, the colours of which exactly matched the colours of her hair.

To say that May and Bella didn't get on together would be as obvious as saying that oil and water are incompatible. May disliked Bella with her loud mouth and bullying ways and Bella was contemptuous of her sister-in-law's pretentiousness. May had "a hoose wi' a back an' front door" and she liked you to know it.

As a rule, in any chance encounter, these two ladies, related by marriage, would exchange little more than curt nods. Bella was surprised therefore when May, who could easily have slipped into the Post Office as Bella was approaching, instead waited for her in the street. Bella, released from the pain and discomfort of the toothache and refreshed by a good night's sleep, was back to her old self again. Cautiously she approached May, "She's up to somethin'," she thought.

"Hallo there Bella, ah've no saw ye fur ages," gushed May, "Is this weather no' just the limit? It wid sicken yer happiness." Not even Bella could argue with that. "Aye, wid it no' just," she agreed, wondering what this was leading up to. "Ah hope it gets better afore the holidays," said May, "Ur youse goin' away this year?" adding casually, "Ah mean together." "What's she up to?" thought Bella then, smiling sweetly she said "Oh ah dare say it'll be Anstruther as usual." "Me an Douglas ur goin' tae Majorca — again," said May complacently. Bella relaxed, so that was it, "She just wants to bum about her furrin holidays," she thought. "That'll be nice fur ye," she said, "Ye've told us how much ye like it — often enough." "Ye've nae idea o' the difference," May simpered, "Once ye've been abroad ye'd never go back tae — " her nose wrinkled in disgust, "- Anstruther." Bella raged within. "Anstruther suits us, the weans like it an' there's some nice wee pubs fur me and Dunky," she said, more defensively than she had intended. "In any case," she continued, "ah've no' got any notion fur tae go abroad." "Whit aboot Dunky?" said May innocently, "It wid suit him." Bella snorted, "Dunky go abroad?" she laughed, "Nae chance o' that, ye couldnae get him to leave Scotland, no' for a million pounds."

Bella smiled at the very idea. May smiled too, the open goal beckoned. "That's no' whit ah've heard," said May coyly. Bella's heart stopped, she realised she'd been outmanoeuvred. A trap had been set and she had walked right into it. "Whit's that then?" asked Bella, a smile stiff on her lips. May affected amazement, "Oh have ye no' heard?" she said, infuriatingly vague. "Huv ah no' heard whit?" demanded Bella, her fists clenching ominously.

It was a long time since May had enjoyed herself so much. "Ah bumped intae Gloria Crawford yesterday," May said, "Ye know Gloria? Knocks aboot wi' Alan McLinder." "Aye of course ah know her," snapped Bella. betraying her impatience. May continued. "Ye should huv seen her, talk aboot mutton dressed as lamb, her skirt hardly covered her backside." Bella fumed, Gloria's sartorial shortcomings were of little interest to her at the moment. "Well anyway," said May, getting back to the point, "Apparently Alan's away tae Lisbon in this auld van he's got. Ye know how he's keen on motors an' that?" Bella knew this of course. "Well so what?" asked Bella dreading the answer. May paused, looking doubtful, "Here maybe it's me that's got the wrong end o' the stick." May had thought to spin things out in this vein for a while but one look at Bella's thunderous countenance warned her of the dangers. "Well the fact is that Alan sent her a postcard an' in it he said that your Dunky wis wi' them," said May blinking innocently.

Bella had prepared herself for some dire denouncement but never could she have anticipated this. "Dunky's whit?" gasped Bella. May's moment of triumph was almost complete. "Of course, as ah say, ah might huv got it wrong. Ah mean if you didnae know Dunky was away tae Lisbon, ah might huv been mistaken," said May, coy and contrite.

What Bella would have given to get her hands on Dunky at that moment. That any women could think such thoughts of the man she had vowed to love, honour and obey was, on the face of it, indefensible, but from Bella's point of view not only had her husband deserted the family home without so much as a word of explanation,

71

this had happened often enough before and was in itself forgivable, but what was unforgivable was that Dunky McLinder born of staunch Protestant stock was, even now, on his way to Lisbon to support Celtic!

Bella was aghast, the shame and the degradation she would suffer if word of this ever got about. How could she face her brothers and could she ever again hold her head high in the Orange Walk on the twelfth of July, even - perish the thought - even excommunication from the Orange Order itself was a possibility. And, as if all that wasn't enough, she had, at this very moment, to suffer this humiliation at the hands of a sworn enemy. Try as she might, there was no way out, Bella knew it, May knew it, May's triumph was complete.

Nevertheless Bella rallied, she still had some pride. "Oh that's where he's went," she said as lightly as her leaden spirits would allow, "Ye know whit Dunky's like, aye jookin' aboot somewhere." A brave reply in the circumstances. "Well now ye know," crowed May, "Well ah'll no' keep ye any longer, ah'll need to get on. Ah've enjoyed wur wee chat." "Ah'll bet ye huv," thought Bella, "Ah'll be seein' ye then," she said with some effort.

May had gone only a few yards along the crowded Main Street when she turned and called to Bella, "Mind an' tell Dunky ah wis askin' fur him - when he gets back frae Lisbon," then smirking triumphantly she minced off like a two tailed cat. May's parting remark had been overheard by upwards of a score of passers-by. Within the hour Dunky's treachery would be common knowledge. Bella, her face burning with rage and shame, glared after her sister-in-law, her feelings at that moment can best be described in the vernacular, "Big Bella was bealin'."

CHAPTER SEVENTEEN

From the early hours on Thursday 25 May 1967 Glasgow buzzed with supressed excitement. Anticipating the principle of flexi-time by a decade and a half, factories and offices were manned almost to capacity two hours earlier than normal. Others who were unable to make an earlier start, worked on uncomplainingly, through lunch and tea breaks. And others again, with a cavalier disregard for their contractual obligations, simply announced that they would be leaving early that night.

Only a very determined recluse would have been unaware of the reasons for this unaccustomed early activity. Weans in prams could have told you, sophisticated spinsters in Hyndland could have told you, and, without doubt, the legion of Celtic supporters and their sympathisers would have told you. The Game was to be televised live from Lisbon starting at 5.30 that evening.

No conversation was complete without reference to The Game, Glasgow was alive, thrilling to the sense of an historic occasion. Spurred by the prospect of glory the city's adrenaline flowed freely, its pulse thrilled with anticipation.

From Abbotsinch Airport on the south side of the city, eleven planes were scheduled to ferry the fans to Portugal to augment the impressive army in cars, coaches and vans, already assembled in Lisbon. In the words of the song: There was going to be a show and the Glasgow Celtic, and their support, would be there.

For the Springfield Regulars in the Tar Spangled Banger it was touch and go for a while as to whether or not they would make it to Lisbon in time for the kick-off.

In the aftermath of their debauch, Dunky had valiantly and heroically overcome the debilitating effects of the drink to ensure that progress was made towards their goal. Without ever approaching the targetted mile a minute, Dunky's progress was slow, steady and careful.

It took Alan until the late afternoon on the Wednesday to overcome the combined effects of the wine and the crack on his skull. After consulting his charts, his maps and his watch, and no doubt taking into consideration, tides, wind changes and the juxtaposition of the galaxies, Alan realised just how far they were behind schedule. Not that the others were worried, far from it. Without exception the Regulars were draped uncomfortably over, under or between the seats, mercifully comatose.

The bruising above Alan's left eye had swollen to such an extent as to leave him with only one effective eye. He was nevertheless determined to reach Lisbon in time for The Game the following day, not only because that was the point of the whole expedition, but because his pride and the self imposed strictures of his imaginary rally demanded it.

Stopping only for a couple of hours on the Thursday morning,

Alan, the Tar Spangled Banger and the Springfield Regulars arrived in the Portuguese capital with an hour and a half to spare.

Fortunately by this time the lads, with the resilience of youth, had thrown off the worst effects of the wine. In fact it might even be said that they had benefited from the experience. Bored with the endless travelling and irritated with each other, the knockout effect of the wine had spared them further agitation and in-fighting since they had been unconscious, or at best only semi-conscious, for the last leg of the journey. They had also incidentally saved themselves the expense of feeding. And now here they were at last in Lisbon and, apart from understandably stiff limbs, fit, able and ready to go. It's an ill wind that has no silver lining.

It was decided that since it was so close to the time for the kick-off that it would be as well to drive directly to the stadium. There had been times during the journey when, so obsessed were they by the minutiae of travel, that the ultimate objective of the trip had been almost forgotten. Not now.

Approaching the stadium the Regulars experienced again the familiar thrill of match day excitement. En route they were greeted like heroes by the local populance responding to the show of green and white favours. Anxious now to be part of the colourful scene, the lads were out of the Banger almost before Alan had stopped. It had earlier been decided that Dunky would get Alan's match ticket since Alan had no interest in football. And so the weary driver, having achieved his objective, sighed an exhausted sigh of triumph and stretched out in his favoured sleeping place in the back of the van.

Accustomed as they were to the building excitement engendered by normal pre-match rituals, the lads were affected by the friendly carnival atmosphere of this occasion. Other Celtic supporters, and they were there in their thousands, were greeted like long lost friends. Here they were, 2,000 miles from home and the scene might be mistaken for London Road on a Saturday afternoon. Only the humid heat from a relentessly scorching sun, the babble of foreign tongues and the dry, sweet, unfamiliar smells of Portugal impressed on them that this was different, this was the big one.

Adding to the excitement and the colour of the ocasion there were the Italian fans decked out in red and black. They too greeted the Celtic contingent like brothers. Smiles and good natured, though mutually unintelligible, taunts were exchanged. The Inter Milan fans were confident, this was the third time in four years that the Milanese

74

side had contested the final. Accustomed to success on these occasions their friendliness was tempered by a haughty contempt for the Scottish pretenders to their crown. Their attitude towards Celtic and their supporters was much the same as the attitude their Glasgow counterparts would have adopted in the unlikely event of Brechin City, for instance, having the temerity to contest a Scottish Cup Final against Celtic at Hampden Park. As far as the Italians were concerned, the Scots were there just to make up the numbers. Happily the fans of '67, with a touching naivety unimaginable in the fans of today, were largely unaware of this air of condescension.

Once inside the stadium the Regulars, used to the towerring terraces at Hampden, Parkhead and Ibrox, were surprised to find themselves looking across at a grassy bank surmounted by a row of cypress trees. They themselves were in the main stand which was a concrete affair, running the length of the pitch, magnificent by any standards. It was almost as though one side of Wembley Stadium had been transported to a public park. Like most continental stadia, which seem to have been designed primarily as athletic grounds, a wide running track surrounded the pitch and, ominously, surrounding the track was a concrete moat. The playing surface itself was immaculately manicured and mown in smart alternating swatches, the turf lush and green.

The Regulars were among the bulk of the Celtic fans seated on the concrete steps which still retained the day's heat. The Celtic supporters joyfully sang their way through their complete repertoire, impressing the locals among the crowd and winning the neutral Portugese over to the Celtic cause. With half an hour to go until the kick-off the excitement and the expectancy inside the stadium mounted minute by minute.

There was still thirty minutes before play started when the Springfield bar opened its door. Normally Thursday night, the night before pay day, was one of the quietest nights of the week. Not so on that particular Thursday. No sooner had Auld Tam, unlocked the heavy front door than he and his staff were inundated by as many as might be expected on a busy Saturday night. With admirable foresight, but in contravention of the law, Auld Tam had had a twenty four inch television set mounted in a prominent position above the bar.

Lest it should be supposed that this influx in trade was due to a dearth of television sets in the homes of the Springfield's patrons, it should be made clear that this was certainly not the case. There would at that time have been few houses in Rutherglen without a TV set, although many of them would still only be capable of receiving but one of the three channels then available and none of them would have been colour sets. The Game however was being broadcast on BBC 1 so the lack of an altenative channel would appear to have been academic, in that no one who wanted to see The Game needed to leave the comfort of his own armchair. But that is to misunderstand the gregarious nature of the football enthusiast and the element of involvement essential to generate an authentic match atmosphere.

As far as the quality of the transmission was concerned, viewers accustomed to the technical wizardry of today's sports programmes would be amazed at the unsophisticated presentation then accepted as normal. The primitive monochrome transmission lacked many of the refinements nowadays thought to be essential. The cameras, for the most part, showed few close ups of the play, nor did they have the facility of instant replays. Concentrating only on long shots of the action, there was a naive tendency to follow the ball while at the same time allowing the viewer to see the relative positions of the other players. In short the play could be followed at home without constant interruption of its natural flow and was the next best thing to actually being there.

It should be pointed out that this too was before the time when craven broadcasting authorities had been persuaded of the necessity to provide separate commentaries for sensitive Scots. Where today would be heard guttural garrulous voices, chosen more for their patriotism than for their ability to read a game, Kenneth Wolstenholm's commentary was knowledgeable and economic and was delivered without a posse of cliche ridden experts.

With half an hour to go until The Game started there remained one important issue which, even at this late stage had still to be resolved. Among the Rangers' fans who frequented the Spring there was a hard core who, notwithstanding the unique importance of the occasion, could not bring themselves to alter the habits of a lifetime, the very idea of giving their support to Celtic was anathema. The majority of their fellows had sensibly not allowed sectarian differences to cloud the fact that this was a Scottish team challenging for the most coveted prize in club football and as such deserved the wholehearted support of the Nation. Stubbornly these diehards had resisted all attempts to persuade them of their patriotic duty, but amazingly, by kick-off time they had been converted. It was Bertie Burns who did the trick.

Bertie had a reputation in the Springfield as being something of an

76

intellectual. Balding, bespectacled and shabbily bohemian Bertie could be found in the public library as often as he could be found in the Springfield bar. Seldom seen without a book, Bertie worked by day for the Electricity Board, prompting an oft quoted quip by Dunky McLinder, "Aye readin' something that yin, he read ma meter yesterday." Bertie, never happier than when in an argument, had often distinguished himself in bar room debates and his opinions were respected.

Bertie's argument in this instance was brilliant in its simplicity. If, reasoned Bertie, they objected to supporting a Catholic team it should be pointed out that there were, as a matter of fact, several Protestants in the Celtic side and one of them, Ronnie Simpson the goalkeeper, was the son of a former Rangers star no less. Encouraged by sage nods from his audience, Bertie continued. Even the great Jock Stein himself was a Protestant. By now resistance was ebbing, Bertie pressed his advantage. On the other hand, he contended, every player in the Inter Milan side was a Catholic, their Manager and all their supporters were Catholic since Italy was a Catholic country. Furthermore, it was reasonable to suppose that all the Italians would be willing Inter to win, and here Bertie played his ace of trumps, and what about his Holiness the Pope? Wasn't he too an Italian and who did they think he would be supporting?

No one could argue with such brilliant reasoning, their duty was clear. Within a few minutes and with a few well chosen words Bertie Burns had convinced them of the righteousness of Celtic's claim on their temporary allegiance. They were grateful to Bertie and marvelled at his perception. Now that it had been pointed out to them they couldn't understand how they hadn't seen it for themselves.

That settled, Auld Tam turned on the TV. It was not yet 5.25 when the transmission was due to begin and there on the screen, since it was a Thursday, they watched the end of the children's programme "Blue Peter". There are some things which never change.

CHAPTER EIGHTEEN

Two minutes later and almost 2,000 miles away the players of Glasgow Celtic and Inter Milan took the field. All football fans will know the nerve tingling rush of emotion when the proud tears sting the eyes at the first sight of the well loved colours on the big occasion.

77

The loyal fervent fans who had moved heaven and earth to be there hailed their hereos, tumultuously they welcomed the Grand Old Team.

Up in the stand the Regulars were thrilled, scarce able to believe they were actually there. Paul, the twins and even Dunky roared like demented banshees. Joe was entraced by the spectacle, drinking in the atmosphere, storing it in his memory for all time. Desmond was damp eyed with the choking joy of the moment.

The ovation continued until play began then, as the fans roared them on, the Celtic side raced into action. With an intensity which matched the fervour of their following the men in green and white attacked from the kick-off. Skilful and swift the Celts dominated the early exchanges. The pattern was established early in the match, the Italians being content to let the Scots do the running, confident in their own infamous ability in defence to keep their goal intact and relying on the speed of their forwards to score on the break.

Jock Stein had naturally foreseen that this would be the case and had instructed his side to watch for just such a ploy. Nevertheless, with only eight minutes gone Inter broke away. An Italian forward was driving ominously towards Simpson's goal when Jim Craig brought him down with a desperate last ditch tackle. Horror struck, blood turning to ice in their veins, the Celtic support saw the referee point to the penalty spot. The spot kick was clinically converted, the unthinkable had happened, Celtic, against the run of play were behind.

Despite the heat of the evening the Celtic fans shivered with the chill dread of the inevitable. Over the years the Italians had perfected the art of negative football, content with a one goal lead they were past masters at killing a game by time wasting tactics, petty fouling and by pulling ten men back in defence. Using these methods the Italians had won many matches but few friends.

For the remainder of the first forty five minutes Celtic laid siege to the Inter goal and although they came agonisingly close several times the inspired goalkeeper kept them out. As the teams trooped off at half time the Regulars were despondent. After all their sacrifices and privations their odessy seemed doomed to end in disappointment.

Back home the nation had followed the drama with sinking hearts. In the Springfield they had seen it all before, Scottish teams who had promised wonders only to be found wanting when it mattered most. As in many another pub and club in the land, an atmosphere of gloom and foreboding pervaded the bar at the interval. Even those diehard

Ranger' fans who, it might be supposed, would have revelled in their rival's discomfort, readily conceded that Celtic were unfortunate to be behind after their spirited first half performance.

As it was in the pubs so it was in the homes too. While their menfolk endured the grim misery of the interval in that distant capital, the Regulars' women suffered too.

Anne Marie had seen little of the play, having spent most of the time attending to her son who had been in a particularly wilful mood. For baby Kenneth it was an inauspicious start to his career as a Celtic supporter.

While Anne Marie was fretting with her offspring, Mrs O'Brien was fretting without hers. Little interested in The Game she watched the television mainly in the hope of seeing her sons in the crowd.

For Jean at least there was some relief now that The Game was in progress. The Portuguese women, for ninety minutes at least, would be spared the attentions of her lustful husband. Oversexed though he may have become, she understood her Desmond well enough to know that his greatest obsession was Celtic Football Club, and if the green and white shirts were anywhere engaged in competition, there too would be Desmond.

Big Bella glowered at the television screen then glowered at her children who were watching it. Every fibre of her being outraged at the inquity of having her offspring watch Celtic in her own home and, worse still, although they knew better than to make this clear, hoping they would win, thus compounding her husband's infidelity. For this was how Big Bella saw Dunky's defection to Lisbon. No greater damage could have been done to their marriage than if Dunky had been discovered in an adultrous association. Even the fact that Celtic were a goal down gave Bella little cause for satisfaction. That lot were dead lucky, it was a well known fact.

Although the TV was on in the Dolan home in Croftfoot, Betty had pointedly ignored the first half action. It was still a contentious point with her that Joe should prefer to follow his silly football team abroad when the money spent on the trip could have provided additional furnishings for their home. Sulkily she nursed her grievance as she unwrapped a forbidden chocolate biscuit. The second half was about to begin and contemptuous of the fuss that was being made about The Game, she watched disdainfully as the players come out again and defiantly savoured the flavour of the Blue Riband.

Nevertheless, however despondent the viewers may have been about

79

Celtic's chances as long as there was hope they would stay glued to their sets willing the Scots to excel. Few folks could be found out of doors that evening between 5.30 and 7.15. In Scotland in general and in Glasgow in particular, the thoroughfares were unnaturally silent and deserted. In Main Street, Rutherglen, mangy dogs skulked suspiciously past dormant stores and sparrows cheekily ruled the roost, swooping with impunity to scavenge between the pavement cracks.

The second half started as the first had ended with Celtic attacking the Inter goal. Time and again the hopes of the faithful were raised by the enterprise of the Scottish side only to be dashed by the deadening defensive tactics of the Italians. But, as the game progressed, the Inter tackling became more desperate, their covering less confident, a tribute to the wiles of Auld and Johnstone and to the tireless running of Lennox, Wallace and Chalmers. The champions of Scotland mounted attack after attack until it seemed inevitable that the Italians would crack. The spectators in the stadium and the viewers at home urged on their favourites desperately as the precious minutes slipped away with nothing to show for their valiant performance. Attacking now on the left, now from the right, cuting the ball back from the goal-line, threading it through the solid defensive wall of black and red shirts, fierce crosses and dainty chips, there was no end to the Celtic invention. Twice the woodwork was hit, at least one penalty claim as good as that awarded to Inter was turned down. But still the Italians held firm, was there no justice?

On the terrace at Lisbon the Regulars, spirits lifted by the performance, suffered countless agonies as time went by without the reward their heroes so richly deserved. In the Spring back home the patrons were absorbed in the contest, noisily and passionately, notwithstanding the two thousand miles which separated them from the actual event, they encouraged the Celts, berated the Italians and slandered the referee.

No one witnessing this exhilerating exhibition of attacking football could fail to be impressed by the Celtic performance, Mrs O'Brien stopped searching the faces of the crowd for her sons and concentrated instead on the play. Anne Marie and Jean were spellbound and even the supercilious Betty was irked by the injustice of the scoreline. In fact so impresive and exciting was the Celtic onslaught that even Big Bella had stopped glowering at all and sundry and was now covertly following the action from the shelter of her kitchen.

Half an hour to go and still Celtic trailed, as each furious attack floundered on the rock of the ten man defence there was ever the danger of an Italian counterattack on the exposed Celtic goal. Breathless nailbiting seconds ticked away, the Italians had weathered the crucial spell after the break. According to their philosophy their opponents would now wilt, spent and exhausted from their vain efforts. But not Glasgow Celtic, not on this night at least.

With twenty seven minutes of the game remaining the Scots mounted yet another attack, this time from the left, the ball was cut back across the line of the penalty box and from there, twenty yards out, Tommy Gemmel crashed an unstoppable shot into the roof of the net.

Deliriously the fans home and abroad hailed the Celtic goal, rescued from the depths of despair they celebrated with unbridled joy. That the mere act of witnessing a plastic sphere, no more than 28 inches in circumference, passing through a rectangular space of 192 square feet can provoke such demented behaviour defies rational explanation. Pity only the man never to have experienced that explosion of jubilation in his breast, never to have been transported to the realms of ecstasy by such a deed. In the context of the occasion, Gemmel's goal is still regarded as one of the greatest goals ever scored.

There was no stopping Celtic now, to their previous enterprise was now added the conviction of their invincibility. Their efforts redoubled, their skill boundless, the Lions of Lisbon roared towards their destiny, inspired and inspiring the rampant Celts surged irresistibly forward.

There was bedlam now on the terraces in Lisbon. The neutral Portuguese, wishing justice to be seen to be done, combined their vocal support with the Scots. In the stadium the Celtic cause lacked nothing in volume and commitment.

At home the nation watched entranced as glory beckoned. There was pandimonium in the Spring. Captivated by that valiant display, even those who had had to be converted to temporary allegiance were now solidly behind the Celts, men who in normal circumstances would only have referred to Celtic players by their surnames qualified by profane or slanderous adjectives, now cajoled and encouraged "Bertie", "Tam" and "Stevie" to greater deeds.

Mrs O'Brien, outraged by the leniency afforded to the increasingly desperate Italians by the referee, decried a particularly diabolical decision citing Christ and his earthly parents as witnesses. Up in

Croftfoot Betty squealed in protest at these inquities. And, wonder of wonders, Big Bella emerged from the seclusion of her kitchen to join her children in front of the telly. The kids, who were amazed by this action, were soon to be astounded. After yet another penalty claim had been turned down they witnessed the incredible spectacle of Big Bella, angry veins standing out on her forehead, eyes blazing with passion, yelling at the set, "C'mon Celtic, get intae thae Tally bastards!"

What chance now had Inter?

With time running out there was ever the chance that the glory, so tantalisingly within reach, could yet elude the Parkhead men. The eternal enemy ground imperiously on, 84 of the 90 minutes had passed and still the sides were equal. The drama was intense, thrilling the faithful fans in the stadium, scarcely was there any respite from the excitement on the pitch. So close, so agonisingly close did Celtic come to that elusive vital score, they wondered even then if it was all to be for naught.

But fickle though fate may be, virtue and valiant effort were to be rewarded. With five minutes to go Steve Chalmers achieved immortality for himself and his team mates when he ended a fluid Celtic move, darting into the six yard box between wilting and despairing defenders to divert the ball past the exhausted keeper. Celtic were ahead. This was the stuff of dreams, a story book ending, yet it was so.

In the stadium, in the Spring, in Glasgow tenements and in inaccessible Highland crofts, home or abroad on land or sea, Scots rejoiced.

Five minutes remained, five teasing minutes bitter sweet with anticipation and dread. But Celtic sure and assured, pretenders no longer, dominated the final stages as they had the entire game. At last the referee blew for time, Glasgow Celtic were the undisputed champions of Europe.

Rapturously, noisily, increduously, the travelling support acclaimed their victorious heroes. Dunky, Paul and the twins, arms entwined in one great blob of joyous humanity, bounced crazily together. Joe, clenched fists punching the air above his head, risked permanent injury to his vocal chords. Desmond wept. Overcome by the emotion of the moment, Desmond, whose perception in other matters was less than total, was fully aware of the magnitude of Celtic's achievement.

Steeped in the tradition and heritage of the club since his first conscious moments, Desmond loved his team, suffering with them in the bad times, exalting in the good. And now, his emotions battered by the magnificence of the occasion and Celtic's majestic performance, he wept, proud happy tears.

The local fans augmented the delirious chanting of the Scottish contingent as the Celtic captain led his immortal side to the victors' rostrum, there to collect the coveted trophy. When Billy McNeil held high the European Cup, Scottish football has known no prouder moment.

There remained the traditional lap of honour. Back on to the pitch came the Celtic team and on to the pitch too came some of the Celtic support. With a combination of ingenuity and foolhardiness they overcame the obstacles between them and the playing area to be with their heroes. Reprehensible and dangerous actions such as these would, quite rightly, be stamped upon today. Fortunately, that glorious night, the Portuguese authorities recognised the innocent spontaneity of the invasion and were content to keep matters within reasonable bounds.

Joe was hard pressed to stop Dunky, Paul and the twins from joining the melee on the field, pointing out how important it was that they should stick together. Eventually and reluctantly they came to see the logic in his reasoning. Enviously the four of them watched the antics of the supporters and players as they ran triumphantly round the ground. Joe too wished he could be among that happy throng. Desmond saw the scene but dimly through his brimming eyes.

Eventually one by one the players departed to the dressing room leaving only Tommy Gemmel, scorer of all important equalising goal, romping joyously amid the fans, seeming determined never to leave the scene of triumph, relishing the exultation and the adulation. And who could blame him or them?

It was almost an hour after the final whistle before the Regulars left the stadium and cavorting crazily along with the rest of the jubilant Celtic support, they danced down the road to Lisbon.

CHAPTER NINETEEN

Back in Glasgow the final whistle had been greeted ecstatically. Blocks of high rise flats were rocked by the tumult of acclaim. In city streets, running like deserted canyons between the towering tenements, startled starlings swarmed heavenward, alarmed by the communal outburst.

In the Spring the noise was deafening, putting the Hampden roar to shame. Patrons and staff alike celebrated clamourously, all were in raptures, some, like Desmond in Lisbon, were in tears, released from the tension of the game, their wildest dreams gloriously fulfilled, their joy was boundless. The game was over, the celebrations were about to begin. It was to be an unforgettable night of revelry, as daft as VE Day, a combination of Hogmany and Fair Friday, celebrated on a balmy May evening.

Restricted by the confines of home or howf, and eager to share their joy, the rejoicing Ruglonians tumbled on to the street. The scenes of uninhibited glee were duplicated throughout Glasgow and throughout the country.

Even Desmond's timid wife Jean was tempted from her hearth. Happily she viewed the proceedings from the closemouth. Jean's heart was lighter now, the burden of depression had been lifted. It had come to her in the course of the match just how silly had been her obsession with the notion of her husband's infidelity, her fears had obviously been groundless, there was only one other love in Desmond's life: Glasgow Celtic. Jean was joined by Mrs O'Brien who was as pleased as anyone by the result. Together they enjoyed the festivities from the sidelines.

Splendidly alone but, to her own surprise, elated, Betty Dolan had even enjoyed the final stages of The Game. Betty had had second thoughts about football being a silly game. It had achieved a more respectable image since Mr Henderson had altered the routine of a lifetime to watch the match, until then she hadn't realised that the staid residents of Clarkston might be interested in football. Infected by the mood of the moment and feeling compelled to join in the celebrations, Betty recklesly devoured the remaining chocolate biscuits.

Anne Marie, determined not to miss the fun, had overcome the restrictions imposed by a dependent child by dressing the infant Kenneth in the green and white outfit he had worn at his father's

84

departure, propped him up in his pram and joined in the shenanigans in the Main Street. Baby Kenneth was an instant hit with the revellers. The high spirited crowds in front of the Town Hall, affected by a collective madness manifest only on rare occasions, danced and sang with gay abandon and long undisciplined conga lines wove insane patterns among sets of reels.

In the course of the evening when the proceedings were well under way, Anne Marie met Big Bella. She was surprised to find Bella participating in the celebrations. "Is this no fantastic?" asked Anne Marie. "Aye ah'm fair enjoyin' masel," said Bella more than a little breathless having just disengaged herself from an energetic eightsome reel. A dazed and diminutive man, who had been her unwilling partner, slumped exhausted against a lamp post with little thought for his dignity, glad only to have survived the ordeal.

"Where's Dunky?" asked Anne Marie, "Huv ye no heard?" said Bella, "He's away tae Lisbon." Big Bella imparted the information with pride. Knowing Bella's prejudices, Anne Marie was amazed. Bertie Burns, the sage of the Spring, was passing at the time, "Noo ye mention it," he butted in, "Ah think ah saw Dunky on the telly."

That exchange took place at about nine o'clock. By half past nine there were few people who had not seen Dunky large as life during the transmission. By ten o'clock it was common knowledge that it had been Dunky who had accompanied Tommy Gemmel on his final lap of honour. Perhaps, had the celebrations continued much longer, Dunky might even have been credited with having scored the winning goal.

The celebrations in Rutherglen benefited from the long light night. With midsummer approaching it was after ten before darkness decended. Over in the Portuguese capital, by contrast, even allowing for an hour's difference, darkness came soon after nine. And with the darkness came the troubles. Until then it had been a night to remember, it then threatened to become an unforgettable experience.

After they had left the stadium the Regulars had mingled joyfully with the crowds heading for the city night spots. En route the infectious cavorting and high jinks of the green and white army had been applauded by the locals who appeared to be almost as delighted by the Celtic victory as the visiting Scots. When the fans chanted in unison "Celtic! Celtic!" the locals joined in, when the fans sang "It's a Grand Old team" they clapped with vigour and when inevitably some

85

supporters danced in the city fountains they smiled indulgently. The spontaneous high spirited antics of the fans of '67 were a world removed from the aggressive yob culture of today's mindless football followers. That there were few complaints about the supporters' behaviour is a tribute to the fans themselves and the sensitive tolerance shown by the civic authorities.

The smell of cooking from an adjacent bistro was sufficiently tempting for the lads to indulge themselves, eating royally at paltry cost, it was their first cooked meal for several days. With single minded determination born of dire experience the wine which was flowing freely all about was shunned by the Regulars. Sensibly they ignored the cheap local wine and drank instead the cheap local brandy.

Truth to tell there was little need for the assistance of alcohol, the victory and the nature of its accomplishment had been a sufficiently intoxicating experience. For that one night in Lisbon the squares rang with guttural Glaswegian conviviality and with inexplicable spontaneity there was born a new Celtic anthem. Starting with the line, "We've got Ronnie Simpson number one," and going progressively through the side and naturally including Jock Stein, it concluded with the punch line, sung with fervour and conviction, "We've got the best team in the world".

Paradise was there under the gayly coloured umbrellas in the warm evening air. Hoarse now and getting hoarser the Regulars joined in the singing with gusto. Nothing, it seemed, could impair the perfection of the moment. It was then that the professional ladies of the town arrived, sensing easy pickings among the elated visitors, many of whom had not been in the country long enough to know one end of an escudo from another. Good time girls there were too, eager to join in the fun, attracted by the joyful atmosphere and the youngbloods among the support. It has to be admitted that there were those who succumbed to the temptation. They were after all only human and who knows, in the way of such things, there may be fair skinned Portuguese now in their twenties with subconscious yearnings for a McGhee's pie or a plate of mince and tatties.

Joe had some trouble keeping the lads together. Bill and Barney, the only two of the Regulars without matrimonial ecumbrance, and whose sturdy frames and boyish good looks attracted attention from professional and eager amateur alike, would almost certainly have been willing victims but for Joe's intervention.

86

Joe advised against involvement on moral and health grounds and Paul, somewhat half heartedly backed him up. Desmond was seen now in his true colours making a mockery of his wife's recent phobia. Cowering fearfully from the blatantly flaunted charms of the most persistent and usually the most generously endowed prostitutes, Desmond urged the twins to be firmer in their refusals. Jean would have been proud of him.

Surprisingly Dunky was apparently unimpresed by the seductive parade of readily available creature comfort. It may well have been the case that his sex drive had been severely blunted over the years by the awesome responsibility of satisfying Big Bella's whims and fancies in this regard. Whatever the cause, Dunky scornfully dismissed such temptations. "Ye'd be wastin' yer time wi' that lot," he informed the O'Briens, "A' the wimmin hereaboots ur Lisbions." Poor pun though it was all the lads laughed, even Desmond joined in — after it had been explained to him.

Nevertheless, despite Dunky's observation there was a marked degree of heterosexuality in the intentions of the Lisbon lassies then in the square, but to their credit the Regulars steadfastly resisted all advances, contributing instead to the impromptu gala concert.

As the warm dusk, filled with twittering darting insects, settled about them, Joe was at peace with the world. Then it was that his world caved in. Just as he had been smugly congratulating himself on having kept his party together, with a heart stopping flash of realisation, he was suddenly aware that that was exactly what he had not done. In the frenzy of victory and in the exciting march on the town, and here in the exotic continetal setting of the square, they had forgotten probably the most important member of the group. Alan McLinder, who they had last seen dossing down in the back of the Banger, was missing.

Consternation replaced jubilation when Joe imparted the dire news to the others. As Desmond perceptively remarked, "Jings, we'd better find him, it's a gi' long walk back tae Ru'glen." "We'll need tae send oot a search party," said Paul. "Me and Bill'll look in the brothels," volunteered Barney with such enthusiasm that a suspicious mind might have suspected an ulterior motive. Joe would have none of it. Successfully he persuaded them to stick together.

Determined to be methodical they first of all made enquiries of the Celtic fans in the square then, drawing a blank, they progressed to the

87

next plaza asking questions on the way and so on through a series of squares each with its own complement of Scottish revellers.

After an hour searching the bars and cafes they had come across several old friends, one of whom had been at school with Dunky and whose home was now less than a mile from his, yet save for that chance meeting in Lisbon two thousand miles away, neither had seen the other for almost a decade. They also met a contingent from Kilsyth, deliriously celebrating a unique double. In less than 24 hours they had seen their local team win the Junior Cup at Hampden in the replayed final against Gelncairn and the Celtic's magnificent triumph in Lisbon. "That's somethin'" as Desmond observed sagely, "That disnae happen every day."

Other faces, vaguely familiar, were spotted among the crowds but, alas and alack, no sign was there of Alan or the Tar Spangled Banger. The discussions to decide which way to search next bacame increasingly acrimonious, the lads were weary now with the accumulated debilitating effects of the journey, the emotional drain of the match and the frustrations caused by their fruitless search. Eventually Dunky, who was less perturbed than the others by their predicament, inclined as he was to random adventures, casually suggested that they make their way back to the stadium since this was the last known sighting of the van. Other options having been tried without success it was agreed to give it a try.

Easier said than done however. None of them had the vaguest idea of the whereabouts of the stadium, in fact, other than that they were in the Portuguese capital, none of them had the slightest notion of where they were themselves. It had been simplicity itself to find the stadium earlier in the day by following the stream of spectators bound for the match, it was an entirely different proposition in a strange city in the dark.

Fortunately after a while they were set on the right road by an English speaking resident. Both parties gained by the encouter, the Regulars were given concise directions and their benefactor added to his English vocabulary a hitherto unheard of form of address. Bidding the lads farewell he eagerly looked forward to the opportunity of impressing his English friends in the town with his discovery. As the lads disappeared into the night he experimented with the exotic new word. "Haw mister," he said, repeating it as he went on his way, perfecting his pronounciation.

The weary Regulars tramped disconsolately out of town, Dunky and Joe in front and Desmond and Paul trailing at the back. These two stragglers, footsore and tired, were just leaving the city centre when Desmond suddenly clutched at his friend's sleeve. "There he is," he cried. "Who?" asked Paul. "It's Alan. he went doon that street there," Desmond said excitedly, drawing Paul towards a dingy alley where the form of a thin man could just be seen in the gloom. They watched as the man disappeared into a dimly lit doorway. "Ur ye sure?" asked Paul, not at all convinced. "Ah'm certain," Desmond replied. "Then whit's he doin' goin' intae a hoose in Lisbon?" Desmond thought for a moment then, remembering a time when Celtic had been playing in Dundee and the lads had been royally entertained by a relative of the twins, he said, "Maybe he's got an Auntie lives there." Paul thought that unlikely and said so. "Ah'm tellin' ye it wis him a' right," insisted Desmond, "Ah'll tell ye what. You go an' get Joe an' the boys an' ah'll go in an' get Alan."

Although Paul was sceptical to say the least Desmond would brook no argument. So, depatching the bespectacled younger man to recall the others, Desmond went down the alley to the dim doorway. The door was open, inside was a small hall lit by a dusty and decrepit chandelier. Two corridors patchily lit by filthy fluorescent tubes ran at right angles from the hall, one straight ahead and the other to the right of the entrance. Directly facing the door an open stairway led presumably to an upper floor and confirming the impression that the place may have been an hotel of some sort there was, only just discernible in the gloom below the stairs, a reception desk and on the wall behind the desk a series of hooks, some with keys hung on them. As testament to the unlikely popularity of the hotel, out of thirty or so hooks, only about half a dozen still had keys hanging on them.

Desmond entered hesitantly, peering along the corridor to his right he saw the man he had taken to be Alan in conversation with a woman at the last of the series of doors. Even from that distance it was obvious that the man had not learned to speak Portuguese in Cambuslang. Preoccupied as he was Desmond failed to notice the figure behind the desk. Clad in a revealing skin tight gold lame dress, her doll like features smothered in make up and topped by an exotic boufant mass of ginger hair, there sat a predatory female form. The ridiculously excessive amount of cosmetics on her face could not conceal the look of bored resignation as she recognised Desmond as yet another football supporter.

"You are looking for a woman?" droned the receptionist. Desmond jumped, "No," he said, squinting down the other corridor still convinced that Alan was somewhere in the building. "Ah'm lookin' for a man." The change in the receptionist's attitude was immediate and surprising, one over elaborate eyebrow arched above her hooded eyes, glinting now with seductive intent. Rising from behind the desk she moved sensuously towards Desmond. Despite the fact that she was head and shoulders taller than himself, Desmond was barely aware of her presence, so intent was he on searching for his friend.

She was behind him when she began caressing his neck. Desmond at first shrugged and ducked, mistaking the caress for the attentions of an insect. When the irritation continued he turned sharply and for the first time he saw the receptionist. Desmond was pertrified. At close quarters, and she was getting closer all the time, she was grotesque. Desmond backed against the wall as the receptionist continued to stroke his neck with one hand while the other, to Desmond's horror, slid over his inner thigh. He was forced against the wall by the advancing receptionist who was so close now that Desmond's head was trapped between her pneumatic breasts.

It was then that Joe and the boys burst into the hallway then immediately burst into laughter. Desmond's desperate attempts to escape the lecherous embrace were comical to behold. The lads made no effort to rescue him from his plight, content meanwhile to let him suffer the consequences of his impetuosity. And yet, amusing as it appeared, there was the feeling of something amiss, something not as it should be. It was Dunky who realised what was wrong. "Wait a minute," he said. "That's no' a wummin, that's a man."

Overcoming their natural distate they hauled the transvestite off their friend. Tottering backwards towards the desk on over high heels, his/her wig drunkenly askew, the homosexual directed a torrent of Portuguese invective at the Regulars. This, combined with the clamour created by the lads, caused doors to open along the corridors. Panic stricken men hastily adjusting their dress, accompanied by women in scanty and erotic garb. The Regulars beat an undignified retreat, dashing down the alley and stopping only when it was apparent there was no one in pursuit.

Still struggling to regain his breath Joe rebuked Desmond for his foolhardiness. Desmond who understandably had been severely shaken by the experience, took some convincing that his assailant had in fact been a man. Desmond considered the matter for a while. "Ah canny get over that," he said at length, his face a mask of incredulity, "That wis a queer kin' o' thing to do, wis it no'?" As Dunky readily conceded, there was no answer to that.

CHAPTER TWENTY

Even when darkness fell in Rutherglen, and that was not until after ten o'clock, there were still scores of boisterous merrymakers on the streets. Reluctant to call a halt to the festivities the crowds eventually broke into smaller groups and repaired to the homes of hospitable folks, good hearted or foolhardy enough to invite friends and neighbours in to continue the celebrations. Differing only from thousands of other such gatherings before or since by virtue of the unique occasion and their impromptu origins, these parties were conducted in the hallowed manner, observing rites and traditions established over many years.

Although alcoholic refreshment was still available, provided by shrewd souls with comendable foresight (they had stocked up at the off-licence five minutes before closing time) tea was served by the ladies of the household and sandwiches, cakes and biscuits miraculously produced.

There was an abundance of goodwill, warmth and friendliness. In smoky homely rooms, cheerfully noisy, old friends renewed acquaintance, while newcomers, wary and restrained to begin with, were soon welcomed into the fold. Taking their chance while their wives busily assisted with the tea things, rowdy, randy men, long married, retold old salacious jokes, slyly testing the reactions of pretty young girls. Those nubile maids, flaunting their femininity, adroitly avoided unwelcome gropings and squealed with affected outrage when liberties were taken which had been artfully contrived. Records were played on the radiogram and dancers amazingly found space to smooch or jive while selfconscious lads boasted boisterously among themselves and convertly eyed the girls. Others, less concerned with the mating game, gathered together to discuss matters of mutual interest, and in shady corners malicious gossip was conducted by crones with severe censorious faces.

When the tea things had been cleared away the party settled down to serious business. "Sit doon here hen, ye've did affy well, ye must be exhausted." In this manner the hostess was thanked for her efforts,

91

ushered to an easy chair and furnished with a welcome drink and a fresh cigarette. The "cairry-oot" having been dispensed and all their glasses charged, the entertainment began, to cries of "Order! Order!" the ball was set rolling by the first singer.

Needing little encouragement, some so eager in fact they had to be restrained with the severe rebuke, "One singer, one song!" uttered with unmistakable menace by sturdy men angered by the breach of etiquette. Shrewd and patient performers there were too who well knew the value of their contributions, no night being complete without this or that idiosyncratic rendition, nor without the comic song, well known to all present but received with such genuine and hearty laughter it might have been newly minted. Occasionally a newcomer would delight with his or her novel party piece but mostly they were tried and tested turns, enjoying exalted status by virtue of their association with these convivial occasions. Great indeed was the variety and the quality of the contributions. Well oiled throats bawled out bawdy ballads with rollicking choruses, crooners crooned plaintive airs, sweet voiced girls sang songs of love and bathroom tenors boomed.

Around midnight their numbers thinned, conscientious types, mindful of the morning's toil, conveyed their thanks and left. Lovers too slipped away, keen to be alone, and grim visaged wives dragged home their reluctant drunken men.

In the aftermath of gaiety the depleted company settled snug and mellow and fondly reminisced and in the wee small hours they sang the old sad songs, the Scots songs and the Irish, the sentimental sobs welled up within them and they knew the sweet rapture of absolute contentment.

It was well into the wee small hours in Lisbon when Joe and the boys finally arrived back at the stadium. Impossible now to imagine that only a few hours ago those same six irritable and exhausted men had been actively and joyfully involved in the victory celebrations. Even after they found the stadium it took another ten minutes or so to locate the correct car park, a process which involved further wrangling and in-fighting and did nothing to improve relations strained close to breaking point.

Already, in his own mind, Paul had broken off diplomatic relations with the others. Pointedly maintaining a distance of several yards between himself and his former friends he resentfully mulled over the injustice of the situation. It had been Desmond after all who had instigated the fiasco back at the brothel and it had been Desmond's naivety which had necessitated the Regulars pell-mell dash in darkened unfamiliar street as a result of which they had lost their way and had been compelled to retrace their steps back to the town centre, thereby adding considerably to the time wasted on a night which should have been spent in uninhibited celebration. Huffily Paul slouched along at the rear wishing he had restrained Desmond, wishing he was in Rutherglen with Anne Marie and baby Kenneth, wishing in fact he was anywhere but in this God forsaken city, treking endless miles and uncertain how or if he would ever get home again.

Nor were any of the others in better temper. Tempers indeed were frayed to such an extent that blows had been exchanged. It began with bickering between Barney and Bill and escalated to the point where Bill struck Barney. Incensed Barney retaliated with such force that Bill was in danger of being seriously injured until Dunky, shocked by the savage assault, intervened and punched Barney full on the nose. Barney howled with pain and toppled backwards. Bill, given respite from the onslaught, looked up to see Dunky hitting his twin brother. In a red faced Irish rage, disregarding Dunky's good intentions, Bill set about his rescuer with flailing fists. Dunky was taken aback for a moment by this painful show of ingratitude then, deciding that attack was the best form of defence, he flung a series of punches at Bill, some of which connected. By this time Barney was back on his feet, outraged that anyone else should inflict on his brother the same punishment that he himself had been dispensing only seconds before, he too physically assailed the unfortunate Dunky. In the course of breaking up the subsequent melee, Joe and Desmond were added to the casualty list, innocent recipients of random blows. Eventually, after a great deal of energy and anger had been expended, the bruised and battered protagonists called an ungracious truce, dusted themselves down and truculently continued their treck.

Arriving at last at the spot where they had so carelessly and with such bright expectations left Alan and their transport their spirits were momentarily lifted when, there in the first light of dawn, was the welcome sight of the Tar Spangled Banger. Their joy was short lived however, when, on closer inspection, it was discovered that the side door was open and, after Joe, an even more reluctant leader than usual, had been persuaded to peep cautiously inside, he dolefully announced that of Alan there was no sign. Once more the acrimonious

93

bickering broke out, each blaming the other for this or that incident, one's lack of foresight or another's intransigence.

But argue as they might there was one indisputable fact, Alan was missing. Speculation as to his whereabouts ranged from the impossible to the impropable. Finally the consensus had it that he had been kidnapped by the Mafia, despite Dunky's insistence that the Mafia didn't operate in Portugal since it was a French organisation.

In the midst of irrelevant, impractical and some downright daft suggestions as to what to do next, the Regulars were suddenly silenced by the sounds of movement in a nearby clump of bushes. Fearful of the presence of nefarious foreign felons or, in Desmond's case, wild lions, the Regulars watched petrified as the bushes parted. Then, to their relief and ridiculously extravagant delight, out stepped Alan.

Still heavy with sleep Alan tugged up the zip of his fly as he emerged from the undergrowth, yawned, stretched luxuriously then, rubbing the sleep from his good eye, he acknowledged the presence of his passengers. "Oh there yis ur, ah wis beginnin' tae wunder where ye'd gone," he said casually. To say the lads were disappointed by this dismissive greeting would be an under-statement, after all their traumas and tribulations it was dispiriting to say the least. Worse was to follow. Heedless of the lads' downhearted reaction Alan proceeded to add insult to their injured feelings. He had lumbered past them walking towards the van then, as the thought struck him he turned, "Oh by the way," he said, "How did yer team get on?"

Since Alan had stepped from the bushes none of the others had uttered a sound. They now broke their silence with a communal gasp of incredulity. For the duration of The Game, Scots the world over had moved heaven and earth to keep in touch with the dramatic events in Lisbon, but here was Alan McLinder, as Scottish as they come, who had been within sight and sound of history in the making, but who had apparently slept through it all.

Alan looked at their crestfallen faces and came to the wrong conclusion. "Oh, like that is it?" he said. "No, it's no' like that at a'," growled Desmond, his pride in his team's achievement overcoming his outrage. "The Celtic won, two-one." Alan looked at the doleful countenances of the others, "Well," he shrugged, "If that's whit yis look like when ye win, ah wouldnae like tae see ye when yis get beat."

The Regulars, truth to tell, were a sorry sight, dishevelled, bruised and battered. They looked at each other and for a moment their despondency deepened. Then, starting with a sheepish smile from Joe, they relaxed and their smiles grew into laughter. The sun was up now, warm and comforting and when they thought about it things were working out well enough after all. Despite all their setbacks and adventures, here they were reunited with Alan and the Banger and, apart from a few scratches and bruises, none the worse for their experiences. And best of all, and most importantly, Celtic were the European Champions.

Alan, refreshed by his long sleep, was keen to get the return journey underway, and since there was no reason to remain in Lisbon, the Regulars, having contributed further to the irrigation of the undergrowth, clambered into the van. Casting last fond glances at the stadium wherein had been enacted such glorious deeds, they set off in the fresh bright sunlight of the new day.

Exhausted by their adventures and lulled by the drone of the Commer's six cylinders it wasn't long before Joe and the boys, well used now to sleeping in the van, were dead to the world, dreaming dreams of home and glory.

In the hazy half life of the subconscious their loved ones beckoned and cooed. Paul saw Anne Marie's sweet face, Joe his bonnie Betty, Desmond beheld his wife and weans. Inhibited by visions of their mother's stern looks of admonition the twins strove to supress lustful longings and Big Bella floated improbably above the crowds in Main Street, seen once again in Dunky's mind's eye, in the pert vigour of her youth. Wafting through those thoughts of home in distorted wraithlike form came friendly sporting Brummie boys, cynical foreign Customs Men with insane lopsided grins, elongated French gendarmes and transvestites, macabre and grotesque. In the eerie echoing soundtrack, a ghostly choir endlessly acclaimed the best team in the world. But superimposed on their mingled memories, etched indelibly in their minds in cinematic clarity, ever and again they saw Gemmel's shot rasping unstoppably into the net.

At the wheel, complacent and serene, Alan playing out his own fantasy, was driving not a beat up old Commer but a custom built rally car. Its engine purring like a pampered pet, The Tar Spangled Banger steamed steadily across the weary miles of the Iberian plain, the Springfield Regulars were homeward bound.

CHAPTER TWENTY ONE

In the week which followed these momentous events, Glasgow was narrowly denied the distinction of being the first city to capture the two premier European trophies in the same season. Rangers were unfortunately beaten in the Cup Winners final by Bayern Munich in Nuremburg, the only goal being scored by the Germans in extra time.

In much the same way as the Celtic fans had flocked to Lisbon did the Rangers' supporters descend on Nuremburg. It is worthy of note that neither in Portugal nor in Germany was it deemed necessary, as it would be today, to activate a full scale red alert against the marauding hoards. Today's tacky tabloids would undoubtedly have discovered, invented or distorted some incident with which to bombast and shock, but, fortunately, this was before the advent of those trite and contemptible scandal sheets.

Late on the Thursday afternoon of that week the Regulars returned to Rutherglen, bade farewell to the Banger for the last time and were happily reunited with their families. Within half an hour of the twins' homecoming, Mrs O'Brien had prepared and served an enormous meal, correctly anticipating their greatest need. Barney and Bill expressed their appreciation by ravenously devouring her cooking.

Paul arrived home as Kenneth was being fed. He was amazed by how much his son had grown in his absence. Kenneth, sated by his meal and presumably overcome by the excitement of his father's homecoming, promptly and obligingly fell asleep. Left thus to their own devices, his parents lovingly made amends for their recent celibacy.

Desmond was given a rapturous welcome by his children until they learned that even if there was such a thing as Lisbon rock, their father hadn't brought any for them. The only momento Desmond had from his epic trip was the match programme which he proudly showed to his family and was surprised and slightly hurt by the scant respect with which it was received. Shyly, after an absence of more than a week, Jean regarded her husband and, unable to quell such disloyal thoughts, wondered how she could ever have imagined him as a

96

ladykiller. Nevertheless, he was her Desmond, familiar and sure. Her eyes glistened as she happily welcomed him home.

Joe had been somewhat apprehensive about the welcome he might receive on his return. He needn't have worried. To his surprise and pleasure Betty was just as delighted as he had been at Celtic's victory. Betty then prepared a meal for the two of them which Joe, who hadn't had a decent bite for upwards of a week, declared to be the best he had ever eaten. Nor was that all. Joe was amazed to be given a choice of chocolate biscuits with his coffee. Then, to cap it all, when it came to bedtime Betty appeared in frivolous filmy baby doll pyjamas in pastel shades of green and white. Privately resolving to recreate these conditions at some future date, Joe passionately entered into the spirit of the moment. Their hearts made fonder by their separation, Joe and Betty were joyfully reunited.

Dunky, who had tentatively entered the McLinder home was surprised to say the least by Big Bella's reaction. Certainly, as was her wont, Bella ranted and raved for a full fifteen minutes, but Dunky, who knew her well, soon noticed that despite the flailing fists and the customary invective, Bella was merely going through the motions. Given the magnitude of his misdemeanour, Dunky wondered at her reticence but was content to play the part of the chastened spouse as etiquette required.

On the day after their return Alan drove the Banger to the lockup, dispassionately stripped the Commer of all its working components tossing them carelessly into a heap of other such mechanical flotsam to be recycled and reconstructed in some other manifestation of his genius. The pitiful remains of the Tar Spangled Banger were then dumped unceremoniously in a nearby scrap yard. The ignominious manner of the Banger's disposal served as a symbolic ending to their adventures. On the same day the Springfield Regulars returned to their work-a-day lives, happy enough to get back to their normal routines, their lives enriched by the experience and the unforgettable memories of the Lisbon trip.